Also by R. Cameron Cooke

Sword of the Legion Series
ROME: FURY OF THE LEGION (Gaul, 57 B.C.)
ROME: DEFIANCE OF THE LEGION (Gaul, 54 B.C.)
ROME: TEMPEST OF THE LEGION (Adriatic Sea, 49-48 B.C.)
ROME: SWORD OF THE LEGION (Egypt, 48 B.C.)

WWII Submarine Novels
PRIDE RUNS DEEP
SINK THE SHIGURE
DIVE BENEATH THE SUN

Other Titles
RISE TO VICTORY
THE CONSTANTINE COVENANT(as Aiden Crisp)

TRAIL OF THE GUNMAN

This is a work of fiction. The names, characters, places, and incidents are either products of the author's imagination or are used fictitiously. Any resemblance to persons, living or dead, events, or locations is entirely coincidental.

ASIN-B071YP6TNC

ISBN-9781521179154

TRAIL OF THE GUNMAN

By

R. Cameron Cooke

My name is Elijah Jones. When I was young, I lived in the age of the gun...

CHAPTER I   The Wild Country

The horses were dead.

Both had been shot through the brain. The flies buzzed heavily around the stiff carcasses. They had been killed recently, no more than a day past, otherwise I might not have come across them. The buzzards circling high above this grove of trees had prompted me to deviate from my path to investigate, and now I wished I had not, for I never liked to see fine horses wasted so, and Carondelet, my own mount, was clearly unsettled by the sights and smells of the gruesome scene.

"Easy boy," I patted the gray fur on his neck, and he seemed to understand I was reassuring him that no such fate would happen to him.

These two ponies had been beautiful beasts, each one a light shade of chestnut, accented by a black mane and white socks. Their deaths had been swift, probably painless, one bullet in the head at point blank range, as one might mercifully end the suffering of a horse that was lame, but these two had clearly not been lame, and it left me wondering why they had been killed.

But then I saw the paint on their haunches, and the way in which their manes had been kept, and the soft, rawhide horseshoes, and I cursed my inquisitiveness. These mounts had belonged to Indians – Apaches probably. A cold chill suddenly crept over me. For, I was a white man hovering over two dead Indian horses. What's more, I was deep in Indian land – and I was alone.

Where there were Indian mounts, there were often Indians, so I quickly turned Carondelet back onto the trail and dragged my mules behind me, continuing on my way as if I had not seen anything.

I was four days out of Silver City, trekking across the vast wilderness of the northern Arizona territory with my horse, Carondelet, and two laden mules. Most folks, when they think of the Arizona Territory, think of barren rock and desert dotted with the fingerlike saguaro cactus, and that would be true were one to visit the vast southern portion comprising the desert basin. But the northern regions, upon the great Colorado Plateau abound with mountains that stretch above the timberline, forests as plush and plentiful as any in Canada, and mountain lakes fed by icy creeks and streams. This was the country of the White Mountain Apaches, a sacred land of incredible majesty and beauty. Anyone who has ever seen it cannot help but understand why the natives cherish it so.

In that country, a man could never feel more alone and under observation at the same time. I had not seen a single human being in three days, the last being a lone trader driving a cart overloaded with salvaged mining equipment. He would sell the scrap in Albuquerque, use the money to load his cart to the brim with luxury items, and then head back across the wilderness to sell the coveted goods in the remote mining camps of the Arizona Territory. Each two-month circuit would produce a nice fortune. Of course, there were risks involved with such work, everything from grizzly bears to mountain lions, from desperate outlaws to renegade Indians. Men who delved in such trade were often a bit odd in the head – and perhaps that was why I was engaged in the same trade. The two mules I towed behind me – named Don Carlos and Ulysses – were loaded down with luxury items purchased with every last penny to my name, and I intended to sell the cherished goods in the Verde River Valley mining camps, to make my own fortune.

Though I had been in this country before, this was a new career for me, an attempt at turning over a new leaf. It had seemed like a good idea after a long bout of drinking in

Silver City, and the sight of the fellow trader had encouraged me somewhat, but each passing day left me wondering if this was the wisest choice for a new occupation. The deeper I penetrated the seldom traversed land, the more I felt like I was being watched. Crossing the green meadows, I felt eyes looking back at me from the darkness beneath the distant trees. When deep in the forest, it seemed the trees themselves stared down at me. When crawling my team along a perilous mountain trail, I could have sworn that on more than one occasion a head had been peering over one of the towering cliffs looking down upon me, only to duck out of sight the moment before I looked. The nights were even worse with the distant sounds of bear and wolf. Needless to say, I seldom slept.

If a man ever wished to feel a closeness with The Creator, this country would fit the bill. I could not help but think of the story from the Bible, taught to me as a child, of Moses traveling far across the wilderness to escape the wrath of the Pharaoh in Egypt. Perhaps, I was not too different from that wayward Hebrew of old. I was leaving my old life behind me, and hoping, at the end of my journey, I would reach my own Promised Land, flowing with milk and honey. To take such a risk alone might seem pure madness now, but life was different then.

It is hard to imagine now what it was like when a man had to brave the elements to move about the country, to look for an Indian behind every tree, to watch for the slightest change in the weather – for your very life might depend on it.

And, of course, a man had to be good with the gun.

CHAPTER II   The Massacre

After leaving the dead ponies behind, I had only ridden about a mile down the trail before I saw the smoke rising above the forest ahead. It was a clear sign that I was not alone in this country. The smoke seemed scattered over a small area, as if from a campsite containing several campfires, and it appeared to be somewhere near the trail ahead, because the dark smudge in the sky drew closer the farther I traveled.

In the hours it took to reach the spot, I concocted several different ideas about what could be the source, but none of my postulations were anywhere close to the truth, nor did they prepare me for what I saw when I reached the base of the towering columns. For there, I came upon a field of death.

Beneath the forest canopy, in a large clearing that had obviously been used as a campsite by more than one group of travelers over the years, lay a terrible slaughter – six bodies, all men, all stripped bare and mutilated horribly. Three or more feathered shafts protruded from each pale corpse. One corpse, the only one not prostrate, had been pinned to a tree by a five-foot-long lance. This weapon looked more ceremonial than warlike, with ornamental feathers and a tip that was crafted from the broken point of an old sword. It was a weapon of a former age, and I had seldom, if ever, seen an Apache carry one.

A dozen mules lay dead across the clearing, all on their sides, many with stiffened limbs pointing grotesquely in the air. A wagon and two horse-drawn carts burned nearby, the source of the smoke. The fires had nearly consumed the hulks, leaving the spoked wheels blackened but otherwise untouched. Clearly, the blazes had been set only a few hours ago, and not long before I had first sighted the smoke.

I had already drawn my rifle from its scabbard. After dismounting, I also removed the tie-down loop from the hammer of my Colt .45 Peacemaker revolver holstered on my right hip. The danger was high, but I could not simply ride on when someone might have survived this tragedy.

As I drew closer to the bodies, I saw bullet wounds as well. Whoever killed these men had made sure they were dead by finishing each one of them off with a bullet to the head. Whether these unfortunate souls had been soldiers, miners, trappers, cowboys, or lawmen, I could not tell, for their clothes had been taken by their murderers. They had all been tortured to some degree. The most prominent of these was the man pinned to the tree. He was an elderly man with white-gray hair. In addition to the lance through his abdomen, his hands had been drawn up over his head and pinned to a tree by a single iron nail. His mouth hung open, his eyes staring blankly at the ground, as if to convey the horror of his final moments.

A man was likely to see dreadful things if he traveled long enough on the plains or in the West. I had seen much in my travels, through the war between the states and the Indian wars - terrible, unthinkable acts committed by both Indians and my own kind, but this killing was one of the most gruesome I had ever seen, and it left me feeling anger against those who had done it. Even if these men had been the most notorious outlaws in the territory, no one deserved to die in such a way.

After searching the camp for any sign of who these men might have been, and coming up with nothing, I decided it was best that I move on. There was little more to be gained by lingering. It appeared to be an Indian raid, perhaps the same Indians to whom those dead ponies a few miles back had belonged. This was, after all, Apache country. But there was something that struck me as odd, something that would not allow my mind to lay the blame so easily.

This had been no small party. It was hard to imagine all these men going down without a fight, and, yet, there was no evidence that they had fought at all. No bullet holes in the trees, no blood on the ground anywhere but near the corpses.

And there was something else. The mules all bore a distinctive brand – a brand that resembled a lowercase "T" with two bars through it. Had these dead men been cow hands from the same ranch? Was this bar "t" ranch somewhere nearby? I did not know of any ranches in Apache land, nor any upon this tract of the plateau. All the towns and settlements for a hundred miles in any direction were down in the basin.

A squawk sounded far off in the woods, a noise that was akin to that of a hawk, but my attuned ears instantly discerned it to be unnatural. I heard the distant neighing of a horse, very faint, but very clear at the same time. Then it stopped abruptly, as if it had been silenced by a human hand. There were wild horses in these mountains, but my instincts told me better. I felt I must not linger, lest I myself end up pinned to a tree.

As I put boot to stirrup preparing to pull myself up into the saddle, something suddenly caught my eye. It lay on the ground beside the tree to which the old man was pinned. It was a hand-sized object and appeared to be made of stained, dark wood which nearly blended in with the mulch-covered forest floor.

After picking it up and studying it, I realized what it was, and suddenly felt like a fool. It was a wooden cross – the kind I had seen hung on the doors of churches or near the altar. These dead men were not outlaws, nor woodsmen, nor cowhands. They were church men. And now the "t" brand on the mules made sense. It was not a "t" at all, but a cross. They belonged to the church. I had been so consumed with the ghastly nature of the scene that I had missed the most telling clue of all.

I realized, at that moment, that the eyes of the old man pinned to the tree stared at the spot where I had found the cross. Perhaps it had belonged to him, and had given him some comfort in his last moments. It was a simple carving, polished through years of contact with oily hands, with no elaborate etchings, save for two long grooves running down each side and a single inscription carved into the traverse. It read *San Miguel*. It was easy to see why the killers had left behind such an unremarkable trinket.

Again, I heard the distant neighing of a horse. My years of experience in such country told me my every movement was being observed, whether by those who had committed the foul deed or someone else. After tucking the cross inside my coat, I knocked some mud off my boots, pretending that had been the reason for my delay. Then I mounted and trotted off as casually as I could, dragging my team behind me.

By the time the sun set, I was far away. I felt guilty about leaving the corpses to the wolves. Those men deserved a Christian burial, but any words I might say over their graves would only serve to corrupt the welcome their souls were receiving in heaven. To say it was a rare occasion when I darkened a church door was an understatement. For I, myself, had sent many a man to the afterlife.

I was a gunman – and a killer.

CHAPTER III   The Ambush

The next morning, I heard the horse again.

The night had been surprisingly uneventful. I had camped with my rifle in my arms, without a fire, leaving Carondelet and the team saddled. I set out again when the blackness above the towering trees turned gray with the first light of the new day, daring to hope the sounds I thought I had heard the day before had been mere whims of my imagination, brought on by my isolation in this immense country – but that was not the case.

I heard the distant neighing again, on three separate occasions, and though I had been riding for hours, it sounded no farther behind me each time. This time of year, these mountains were rocked by thunderstorms almost every day, at the same time of day, and the last time I heard the horse in the distance, it was intermixed with the rumble of an early afternoon thunderstorm. Whoever rode that horse was undoubtedly following me. Running was not an option. While Carondelet was swift of foot, the mules limited my use of his speed, and I was not about to leave them or their valuable cargo behind.

Off to the right, the forest ascended gently to the summit of a low hill. It was not ideal, but it would have to do. I spurred my mount to a gallop, and left the trail, playing out slack that the mules might follow more easily. I was an old soldier of sorts, having served in the crew of a riverboat during the war. From the Cumberland, to the Tennessee, to the Mississippi, I was on the offensive side of more sieges and artillery barrages than I'd like to remember, but there were many times when I fought on land, side-by-side with the soldiers whenever the rebel raiders would make an attempt on one of our naval depots. Any old soldier will tell you, when outnumbered, seek higher ground. I did not know if I was outnumbered, nor if those who followed me were old soldiers, too, but the hill would give me a decided advantage.

Carondelet climbed the hill rapidly, prompting the mules to do the same. The clouds were forming dark and menacingly above the treetops. If luck was with me, the confusion brought on by the brilliant flashes of lightning and the clapping echoes of thunder would mask my break from the trail.

I found a small cropping of moss-covered rocks that would suit my purpose as well as any fort. Loading my jacket pockets with cartridges and percussion caps for my rifle, and grabbing one of my saddle bags, I hitched my team to a tree that would be well within my sight, but far enough away so as not to give away my position, pulled my rifle from its scabbard, and dashed for the rocks. I knew it would be some time before my pursuers realized I was no longer on the trail. If they were any good, they would backtrack and find the spot where my tracks had diverted. If they were really good, then they would surmise what I was doing, dismount and ascend the slope on foot, to make little noise and provide me with as small a target as possible. For, if they came at me mounted, I could easily spook the horses into scrambling back down the hill with a few well-placed shots.

While waiting to for my pursuers to walk into my hastily arranged trap, I checked my weapons. The Bowie knife would remain in its sheath, lest the shimmering polished blade give away my position. My revolver was fully loaded, the quiet clicks of the well-oiled cylinder strangely soothing to my ears. The bulbous heads of the .45 caliber bullets loomed in the chambers like ominous executioners waiting their turn to deliver death. The black steel married to my hand like a custom-made glove, and it was nearly an extension of me, I had grown so accustomed to it. It had seen much use in the two years since I had bought it from that half-Navajo gunsmith in Santa Fe, but I had kept it well, caring for it like a child. But after another careful examination, I holstered it. It would be used only as a last resort. This terrain called for the rifle. The long gun was not as new as my side arm. The walnut stock was cracked in several places, the long blue barrel marred by a series of chinks and a deep scar left there long ago by a Mexican desperado's sword, which I had deflected only an instant before the blade would have split my skull in two. Like my six-gun, the rifle had been manufactured by Colt. It was an 1855 Model .36 caliber revolving carbine, and though it did not look impressive, it was the only thing I still had from that unfertile farm in Kentucky where my father had tried carving out a piece of America for his family, and had failed. The rifle had belonged to my father. It had put food on our sparse table, and had often kept us from starving.

Now, it put men under the ground.

Like a soldier poised in the embrasure of a fortification, I set myself up in a nook between two boulders, doffed my hat and rested my long gun on a natural cut in the rock. I scanned the trees down the slope, searching for any movement. I waited, and waited, all the while trying my best to ignore the flashes of electricity in the dark sky above me, and the angry claps of thunder that served to remind me I could be struck down by one of those bolts at any moment.

It was not long before my waiting paid off. About two hundred yards down the slope, I saw movement, a dash of unnatural color amongst the endless tree trunks. It was a man, crouching low, moving cautiously, a rifle held low at his waist. Another appeared to the left, about fifty paces from the first, and yet another to the right, also about fifty paces from the middle man. They were well spread out, each creeping from tree to tree, looking slowly from side-to-side, evidently aware that they should be cautious. As they drew closer, I saw headbands and face-paint, like I had seen worn by Apache war parties. If these were indeed Apaches, and I could see them so clearly, it meant they either wanted to talk peace, or they were distracting me while other warriors circled around behind me.

Glancing over my shoulder, I took comfort that Carondelet, Don Carlos, and Ulysses had not budged from where I had tied them. They had been through too many thunderstorms to be frightened of the thunder, but I would expect them to act nervous should they catch the scent of an Apache sneaking around behind me.

I have faced Indians before, skilled in the ways of quiet fighting and ambush. They were trained warriors from the day they entered manhood. Only a few years ago, the Apaches of these parts had been at war with the United States, and had often made their living raiding towns in the Arizona Territory and across the border in Mexico. They were not to be trifled with. In this kind of country, I would never choose to face an Apache over a white man, but the tactics being used by the Indians to my front had me puzzled. Apaches did not march up a hill in line abreast like a Civil War regiment advancing on the enemy – at least, not that I had ever heard of. And it had been some time since the Apaches, or any Indians for that matter, had attacked a party as large as that of the church men. We were, after all, in a period of peace – or so the U.S. Government claimed.

As I watched the figures slowly ascend the hill, it was clear to me they did not know exactly where I was, just that I was somewhere nearby. They moved with an odd posture for Apaches, like men uncertain of what they were up against. Clearly, they had seen my tracks leave the trail, but they seemed to have lost them in the carpet of pine needles. An Apache would have had no difficulty tracking my every movement through any terrain. But my puzzlement was put to rest when a brilliant flash of lightning lit up the whole area, and I finally got a good look at the face of the man to my front. He was a white man – a white man adorned in Indian garb. A closer examination of the other two revealed that they, too, were white men. After a moment of pause, while I digested this revelation, it was all suddenly very clear to me. I knew what kind of men I was facing, now, and how I must deal with them.

As I peered through the crevice between the rocks, the men on the flanks soon passed out of my line of vision. The man to my front, however, was clearly visible. I had a clear shot, and could not miss, and so I decided to wait until he drew closer.

The first rule of survival in the west was to avoid a fight whenever possible. These men had not yet done anything to me, except follow me through the woods. If a fight could be averted, I would let them go, but their persistence was convincing me more, with each passing second, that they wanted me dead. Of course, there was always a chance they would give up and go back down the hill. Any hope of that prospect vanished when I heard one of the men on the flanks holler to the others.

"There's his team! Watch out! He's got to be close by!"

They had seen Carondelet and the mules. I knew now they would not stop until they had found me. The man to my front was nearly at point-blank range, but, surprisingly,

24

he had not yet seen me. I decided not to wait for that to happen.

The thunder had been steady for quite some time now, each new thunderclap only a minute or so after the last. And so, I waited. I waited for the expected flash of lightning, counted two seconds, then squeezed the trigger.

My rifle discharged nearly simultaneously with the next clap of thunder. An instant later, a black hole appeared squarely in the center of the man's head. His eyes went blank, and he fell backward, dead before he hit the ground. The other two probably would've continued on for several more seconds without even realizing their partner had fallen. However, the dead man, in his final spasms, must have squeezed the trigger on his rifle. It went off with a jet of white smoke, a sharp crack that occurred well after the last echoes of the thunder had subsided.

There was no doubting his associates were alerted to my presence, and now my own survival was a question of speed. There would, undoubtedly, be a moment of confusion while they came to the full realization of what had happened to their partner, that he had not simply stumbled on a rock, but had, in fact, been shot dead. I decided to take advantage of that instant of uncertainty.

The cylinder of my rifle rotated as I pulled back the hammer, bringing a loaded chamber in line with the barrel. I popped up from my position between the rocks to face my opponents. The man to my right was closest, no more than thirty yards away. The one on the left was more than twice that distance. I swung my rifle around at the one on the right, a medium-build man with a round gut and a soft face smudged with unbefitting war paint. He had seen me too late. I steadied my sights on him for an instant, and fired.

I had fired without taking careful aim. Outnumbered as I was, speed was more important than accuracy. I watched the pudgy man long enough to know that I had struck him somewhere in the torso. He cried out in alarm, firing his gun involuntarily, and stumbling back behind the cover of a large pine tree. I heard a sound like glass breaking, and, out of the corner of my eye, saw Carondelet in the distance, skittish and pulling at his hitch. Don Carlos and Ulysses were braying nervously, spooked by something. The fat man's bullet must have struck near them, and I could only pray none of them – most of all Carondelet – had been hit.

These thoughts coursed through my brain as I whirled around, advancing another chamber on my carbine to confront the other man. At roughly seventy yards, he was already drawing a bead on me as my rifle came to bear on him, and our weapons discharged simultaneously. Through the pall of smoke I saw bits of bark fly off a tree trunk six inches from his head and knew I had missed. His bullet ricocheted off the rocks two steps in front of me. Diving back behind the rocks, I cursed the distraction of Carondelet and the mules that had no doubt led me to miss.

This was not an ideal situation. I had one man behind me, his condition unknown, and another man in front of me, uninjured, who was good enough with the rifle that I should be wary of him. I did not consider reloading my three empty chambers, the long reload time being one disadvantage of my rifle. But three balls still rested on the black powder in their chambers, ready for use.

I was well-hidden from the man in front of me but not from the man behind me. I turned around to check to see that he was still taking cover behind the trunk of the pine tree. He leaned up against it with his back to me, only his arms visible. I had evidently wounded him badly enough that he could no longer hold his rifle, because I saw his right hand draw out his six-gun and hold it upright, pointed at the sky. He stayed in that position for several seconds, as if he were counting down to the moment he would swing around the tree and discharge the gun at me, if not to hit me, at least to distract me while his comrade closed in. And so, I took the opportunity given me, as I had learned to do in countless gunfights in the course of my life.

I leveled my carbine and fired.

It was an easy shot. My bullet passed through his hand, knocking the gun from it. He cursed out loud. And then drew his arms in behind the tree. I did not expect to have any more trouble from him – at least for the time being.

Something told me my other opponent would not be dealt with so easily, and this twice-shot fool behind the tree had given me an idea. It was an old trick, one that would never have fooled an Indian, but this man in front of me, like his companions, was no Indian.

I struck the barrel of my rifle against the rock, not particularly hard, but hard enough to make a loud display of it, as if I were maneuvering behind the rock and had tripped. I wanted to set my opponent's mind on my rifle. The boulder that hid me from him was nearly as tall as a man and some fifteen feet across. I had a choice of covering the right side or the left. It was too big to cover both. I hoped my attacker would conclude the same thing.

Making my way to the right side of the boulder, I nudged the muzzle of weapon out beyond the outcropping, just enough so it would be visible to my opponent on the other side. He might still be seventy yards away, as when I last saw him, or he might have used the moment I was taking care of his friend to close the distance considerably. There was no way for me to tell, short of sticking my head out where it might immediately catch a bullet. I left my rifle lodged in the same natural cut I had used to watch the three men ascend the hill, propping it there and securing it with a large rock, so that it appeared I still held it. Then I drew my six-gun, moved to the left side of the boulder, and waited.

As I saw it, unless my opponent happened to be carrying a stick of dynamite or a hand grenade – like those we had often used to dislodge the entrenched rebels during the war – he would have to move closer to get a clear shot at me. If he saw the barrel of my rifle poking out from the right side of the boulder, he might be prompted to try his luck moving around the other side – where I now crouched, my handgun at the ready. The closer he got, the better for me. For a six-gun was always the better choice at close range.

But this man was not that foolhardy. He had changed positions, skirting in a wide arc around the boulder but still near fifty paces away. I saw him farther up the hill, as he dashed from one tree to the other. He saw me at the same time, and paused for the briefest moment, the hard shock evident on his face. Clearly, he had expected to see my back as I peered around the opposite side. Instead, he found himself looking directly down the sights of my pistol.

In a gunfight, to hesitate is to die. He hesitated, and he died.

The distance was too far for me to be precisely sure of my shot, so I emptied four chambers in rapid succession, in the same time it took him to get off one round. When the smoke cleared, I saw my opponent holding his hip. At least one of my bullets had hit him. He had fired his rifle errantly, but he still held it, and instead of seeking cover, he chose to exert himself in pumping the lever to advance another round into the breech. In his wounded state, he moved slowly, allowing me to take an extra moment to check my aim before I fired again. My pistol discharged, its single percussion like the final note of an orchestral performance. A stream of red ejected from his neck as the speeding lead sliced through the artery there. The rifle fell from his hands. He put his hand to his neck, staring back at me across the distance with confused eyes, less cognizant with each passing second as his lifeblood pulsed between his fingers. The next moment, he collapsed, dead.

As if symbolic of the morose scene, the rain began at that moment – giant drops that pattered off the rocks and disturbed the pine needles at my feet. In the time it took for him to die, I had already reloaded my revolver, the droplets sizzling on the hot, black barrel. I was certain the fight was over, but past experiences had taught me never to put faith in that assertion. For I had once seen a man gutted by a "dead" Indian who hadn't moved a muscle in over an hour.

I had killed two outright. They would never move again. A third groaned in agony, his back still against the tree. I had not seen any others. Then, suddenly, I heard the clatter of hooves of down below the hill. There was a fourth man, and he was escaping.

"Run, Jesse!" The wounded man gave a guttural shout. "Run tell the sheriff!"

I snatched up my rifle and leapt up onto the boulder, scanning the terrain below. I got a good look at Jesse as he crossed the meadow below at a full gallop, pulling the horses of my three victims behind him. So much for honor among thieves. He did not look back, not even once. The rain was increasing in intensity, and visibility was getting worse. I had to hurry. Lining up Jesse in my sights, and judging for the distance and the wind, I was a heartbeat away from squeezing the trigger when something made me pause, something about the fleeing man's deportment. Then I suddenly realized I was not looking at a man at all, but an adolescent boy. There was a youthful, loose manner in which he sat the saddle. Unlike his friends, he did not wear the garb of an Apache, only dingy cowboy clothes, a stained coat, and an equally-weathered, wide-brimmed hat that appeared too big for his head.

I decided to let him go. I would not kill a kid.

The natural stimulation of the fight was rapidly dissipating within me. I could see that the man behind the tree was in no shape to fight. I would deal with him in a minute. First things first.

I examined Carondelet and the mules, gave them a good looking over, and found the only casualty of the wounded man's errant bullet was my left saddlebag, which now bore a long, jagged hole running down the canvas flap. A rivulet of liquid ran out onto the ground. It was not Carondelet's blood, but something only slightly less heartbreaking. I lifted the flap to confirm my worst suspicions. The pouch was filled with broken glass, the remnants of my last precious bottle of whiskey – a good bottle, too, Kentucky whiskey, that had set me back a few pennies.

If there ever was a time for a drink.

With caution and anger, I approached the man behind the tree. He was badly wounded. The first bullet had hit him in the abdomen, which he clutched with a bloody hand, deprived of two fingers by my second bullet. He writhed in agony as the rain washed the blood down his outstretched legs, but I held no sympathy for him.

He was in too much pain to crawl away, or to be any serious threat, so I holstered my gun and knelt such that I was hovering over him. Looking up at me, he saw my face set in mild amusement, and instantly his pained expression was intermixed with anger.

"You get your fancy watching me suffer, mister?" he grunted.

"You and your pals should know all about that," I replied.

"What do you want from me, mister?"

"Let's start with your name."

He looked up at me with bloodshot eyes, hesitated for a moment, and then his good hand dashed feebly inside his jacket, coming out again holding a small, double-barreled derringer. But he was weak from loss of blood, and I easily snatched it from his hand.

"There's your gun," I said, holding the small weapon before his eyes. "Now where's the knife?"

He looked at me puzzled. "I don't know what the hell you're talking about, mister. I got no knife."

"I think you do," I said, picking up a nearby stick and nudging it close to his wound. "I'm talking about the knife you and your pals used to carve up those churchmen. Where is it?"

"I tell you, mister, I ain't got no knife!"

"Then maybe one of your friends has it. Maybe that boy. What was his name...Jesse?"

"You leave him out of this, mister! D'you hear?" The man grimaced. "He didn't do nothing!"

"That's where you're wrong, my eight-fingered friend," I snarled, pressing the stick to his wound. "Little Jesse's already in it, up to his ears. You and your friends saw to that when you decided to bring him along! You're a pathetic excuse for a man, leading a young'un astray. You ought to be strung up!" I took the stick away and waited for him to finish screaming. "Now, if you see fit to repent of your errant ways, and tell me just who the hell you are and just why you slaughtered those men back there, and why the hell you tried to kill me, then I might just let you live."

He stared up into my eyes with cold defiance. "You are meddling in matters you shouldn't, mister. Meddlers don't last long around here -"

I jammed the stick back into his wound, and he screamed again. "But that's not what I asked you. So, let me make it clear. You and your pals are in Indian getups, but you ain't Indians, and when a white man dresses up like

34

that, it means he's doing some mischief, and he wants to lay blame on the Indians. You know what I think? I think you and your pals killed those churchmen and set it up to look like Apaches did it." Despite the pain he was in, I could see in his eyes that I was hitting close to the mark. "And then you wanted to kill me. And why would you want to do that? Did I come upon the scene too early, maybe, before you and your cutthroats were done? Did you try to kill me because you were afraid I might have seen you?"

"None of that matters now, mister." The man laughed boldly between winces. "We don't need them to think Apaches did it now. They're going to think you did it, and that's exactly what Jesse is going to tell them. You can't hide, mister. Sheriff Hobson don't mess around with murderin' gunslingers. You'll be hanging high before the week is out. You never should have put your nose where it don't belong."

I turned the stick some more, and he cried out in pain. "Maybe if you holler loud enough, your friend will come back and I'll have a full bag."

"Go to hell!"

"Not before you, friend!" I snarled.

Throwing the stick away, I forced the muzzle of the derringer into his mouth, cocked the hammer, paused to watch his eyes grow wide with fear and disbelief, and then pulled the trigger.

I told you I had not darkened the door of a church in many a year, and there was good reason for it. I was a vengeful man in my youth. There are three things I could not abide back then, nor now: the abuse of women or children, the killing of an innocent man, and a grown man who leads a child astray. In my experience, outlaws are not born, they are made. Like any craft, the apprentices are led to their fates by their masters. They are directed to a life of crime by either circumstance or a negligent mentor. And what could be more negligent than showing a youth how to kill and torture a band of unarmed churchmen?

At that moment – the moment I blew a hole through the head of that bastard – I wanted revenge; revenge for the dead churchmen, for the old man who had suffered unspeakable torture, and for the trouble this bastard and his friends had put me through.

Killing him was a mercy, really. It was a two-day ride to Dougson. The gut-shot bastard would have suffered terribly and probably would have died in the end. Young Jesse had ridden off with his horse, and I wasn't about to unload one of my mules to carry his worthless carcass.

Besides, that bastard had come close to killing Carondelet – and had shot my last whiskey.

CHAPTER IV   The Apaches

The Territory of Arizona is divided diagonally by a great plateau called Mogollon, rising some two thousand feet above the desert basin and spanning several hundred miles. Above the plateau live plush forests of ponderosa pine, snow-capped mountains, and a vast steppe. Below the plateau, foothills laced with pinion pine and juniper, descend gradually amid rocky vistas and fields of immense boulders as the temperature rises. Finally, far to the south, the foothills meet the ominous Sonoran Desert, a vast, arid wilderness stretching all the way to the Mexican border, and hundreds of miles beyond, where many souls have met their ends under the searing sun.

In most places along the edge of the Mogollon plateau, one encounters sharp cliffs, sheer drops of several hundred feet or more, where a man might grow dizzy gazing past the toes of his boots at the valley two thousand feet beneath him. There are, however, a few passages where ancient landslides have cut steep, although manageable, descents into the rocky precipice. The wagon trail I was following took me to one of these passages, where I found a narrow road with sharp turns, zig-zagging down the slope until it appeared as only a tan-colored line that disappeared into the forest far below. The patchy clouds overhead cast irregular shadows across the basin before me, as far as the eye could see. Far in the distance, a blurred column of gray connected the cloud to the earth, a roaming thunderstorm, drifting across the valley like a squall moving across the sea.

I kept a wary eye out as I rode along the rim, approaching the twin rocks that marked the beginning of this treacherous path. If the boy Jesse wished to ambush me, this would be the perfect place to do it. But when I rounded the rocks to start my descent, it was not Jesse, nor outlaws, that I encountered, but Indians.

Sitting across my path was a band of five Apaches. They were all braves, all bedecked in war paint, all holding rifles. I was startled, to say the least, but I managed to remain calm. Though their faces were grim, I knew they had no desire to kill me – at least, not yet – otherwise, I would have been shot before ever even seeing them.

I reined in and kept my hands away from my guns. There was no sense in giving them a reason to kill me.

"Hello," I said, after a long, uncomfortable silence

The oldest-looking of the group, a man with a dark, creased face, looked me up and down with severe, judgmental eyes. A red headband was tied loosely around his forehead, containing locks of gray hair that lighted upon the shoulders of an open red vest worn over a cotton tunic. He studied my face as if he expected to recognize it, but clearly did not. His eyes then wandered to my over-laden mules, and I decided to try to communicate again before he got any ideas.

"Ya'ateh!" I said, this time speaking in the Apache tongue, for I knew a little.

The older man, whom I shall call Red Vest, kicked his horse out in front of the others.

"You no work for Maha-neek," he said bluntly, almost as an accusation. He had some mastery of English.

I had never heard of Maha-neek before. I had no way of knowing if Maha-neek was an Indian chief, a rival clan, or perhaps some denigrating label applied to white men. Nor did I know whether my association with, or ignorance of, Maha-neek would condemn or exonerate me. But, in my experience, it was always best to be honest when dealing with Indians.

"No," I replied. "I have no knowledge of Maha-neek. My name is Jones. I come from far away to the east."

The braves then conversed amongst themselves for several minutes before Red Vest addressed me again.

"A fool travels through Apache land alone."

"I understood this territory was free passage for all men, whites and Apaches, so long as one does not offend. I mean you no harm. I am on my way to Dougson, just passing through."

"White eyes follow treaties only when it pleases them," Red Vest said sternly. When I returned a blank stare, he added, "Two ponies were stolen from our village three nights ago. Stolen by white-eyes."

It was now clear to me who the dead ponies belonged to, and why these Apaches were painted for war.

"As I said, I'm on my way to Dougson. I want no trouble."

"All white eyes are the same. They break treaty, and then blame the Apache for it."

While I knew there was much truth in what he said, and that the treaties, thin as the paper on which they were written, had been broken several times by Indian-hating white men, there had also been times when Apache war parties had delved out their own brand of hatred. I decided, given the situation, it was not prudent to argue the point with him. It was not my way to apologize, especially when

I had no part in the offense, but I thought this might be a good time to make an exception.

"I'm no thief," I said firmly. "I don't steal from any man, no matter the color of his skin. My heart is troubled that some of my own people would steal from the Apache. I pour my heart out in apology for what they have done."

The hint of a smile crossed Red Vest's face, leading me to believe he was either satisfied with or entertained by my answer. But that sentiment was not shared by all his companions. One of the younger braves, a lean, muscled warrior, scowled at me as though I were a piece of mule dung. In one arm, he cradled a long, rifled-musket of an older model, old enough to have been used in the war – not the war between the states, but the war with Mexico. Despite its age, the weapon appeared to be in pristine condition, and I gathered the young Apache took great pride in it.

The brave, whom I shall call Long Musket, walked his horse behind me as I conversed with his leader, as if my apology and anything I had to say did not matter. He began taking an interest in my mules, first scanning them, then lifting the canvas to see what they carried. He did it with a confident, challenging air, as if there was nothing I could do about it. He was trying to get under my skin.

"Please tell him I don't like that," I said to Red Vest firmly. "These mules and everything on them belong to me."

Red Vest looked at me in disbelief for a few moments, as if he was uncertain he had interpreted what I said correctly. When he saw my face set in determination, he appeared slightly amused and relayed the message to the young brave. Long Musket looked at me with hatred, at first, and then broke out into a maniacal laugh. He maneuvered his horse such that he was knee-to-knee with me. Looking into my eyes with a cold black-eyed stare, he said something that sounded very insulting though I didn't understand a word of it.

"He says, the white-eye squawks like a mating quail," Red Vest interpreted. "He says he could kill you. The mules would then belong to him. Your coat, your hat, and your guns would also belong to him."

I got the impression Red Vest had chosen to leave out some of the more vulgar insults. Whether it was because there were no English equivalents, or he was attempting to assuage the hostility of his hotheaded protégé, I could not tell.

Perhaps Long Musket interpreted my caution as fear, because he seemed pleased with himself, flashing a set of teeth that made him look devilish when taken with the lines of war paint across his face.

"I understood that, among the Apache, warriors honored other warriors." I looked him squarely in the eye. "Stripping the dead is women's work. Are you a woman or a warrior?"

The smile had vanished from Red Vest's face, and he appeared hesitant to interpret what I had said, as a man holding a match near a fuse.

"Tell him that!" I prompted. "All of it."

As the older Apache translated my words, Long Musket's grin faded. He grew visibly more incensed with each passing moment, a deep, simmering rage, for I had insulted his honor.

His hand went to the knife sheathed at his waist. I covered my own knife as well. I did not dare go for my gun. That would've been suicide with the four others nearby. They would not sit idly by while I gunned down their fellow tribesman, no matter how much he had been the instigator. A knife fight was a fair fight, and I knew it was my only chance.

We sat there for several long seconds, staring each other down, our hands locked to the hilts of our blades.

"Does he wish to fight me for them?" I said to Red Vest finally. "Or can I go about my business?"

As the words were relayed, I saw a flash of trepidation cross Long Musket's face, the comprehension that he had placed himself in a bind. For he could not back down now and save face before the others. He was committed to challenging me to individual combat, and he had clearly not expected that.

Red Vest spoke in an admonishing manner, as if he was disappointed, not in me, but in Long Musket for causing the whole incident. But, no apology or excuse could stop the events now in motion. In the world of the white man, as well as the Indian, honor was everything. Like two medieval knights exchanging gauntlets, neither of us could or would back down. Only blood could settle our differences.

I hitched Carondelet and the mules to a tree, stripped off my coat and shirt, hung my gun belt from my saddle, and drew out my Bowie knife. Long Musket waited for me at the edge of a circle drawn in the mulch by one of the other warriors. The young warrior now brandished his own blade, a sinister weapon that resembled an ice pick more than a knife. He held it with the blade reversed in his hand. This was a good technique. It allowed one to punch his opponent as well as stab, and it was the posture I assumed as well.

The rules did not have to be explained. It was clear we were to stay within the circle or the other warriors who now stood around it would shove us back inside. Long Musket said many things in his language, all of them meant to taunt me, but fear was a language understood by all men, and his threatening invective only revealed to me that he was nervous and trying to talk himself into some courage.

We started at opposite ends of the ring, and Long Musket wasted no time in attacking. With a shrill war cry, he charged me, and I moved only just in time to avoid taking the point of his weapon deep into my shoulder. The quick side-step threw me off balance, and I tumbled to the ground. He came after me in my disadvantaged position, stabbing downward multiple times in rapid succession. I rolled away from him again and again, just escaping each reaching stab.

The other warriors laughed as he chased me around the circle, clearly amused to see me rolling in the dirt to get away from the deadly sweep of his blade. At one point, he over extended himself, expecting me to roll again, and I took the opportunity to bring my leg around and kick him in the face as hard as I could with the pointed toe of my boot. His nose crushed under the impact, erupting in a spout of blood as he fell to the ground reeling in pain. This momentary reprieve allowed me to get back on my feet, which I did in a flurry of dust, and prepared to meet his next attack properly. But he did not come at me immediately. As he stumbled to his feet, I could see that his nose had been savagely smashed. Nose wounds bleed badly, and his was no exception. His mouth, chin, arms and torso were a mix of blood and dirt. He must have been in enormous pain, but he did not cry out. He wasn't taunting me anymore, neither were his comrades laughing. When he finally advanced again, I was ready. Crouching low, I met his onrush, batting his knife arm out of the way and striking him hard in the right ear with my closed fist. He took that blow well, like a brick wall, and immediately swept his knife behind him, hoping to catch me in the ribs. But I was ready for that, too, and slashed at his forearm, opening a five-inch gash before withdrawing my blade.

Again, we separated, him to escape a deadlier stroke, and me to prepare for his next charge. As we stared at each other across the circle, I could see the stark comprehension registering on his face. He realized I was not unskilled with the knife. What he could not have known was that I had spent my time in the war, serving as a deck hand on a river ironclad, living side-by-side with some of the meanest, dirtiest scoundrels one could imagine. Those hot, muggy, mosquito-infested days on the rivers of the deep south were miserable enough to set men's tempers flaring. Add to that an ample supply of confiscated spirits, and you had a dangerous combination. Fights broke out often, the more serious ones often taken to the sweltering, dimly-lit boiler rooms, where the fighting space had often been more confined than this circle. I could honestly say, I'd rather face five Indians in a knife fight than one riverboat man. With most Indians, you might get a fair fight. Whereas, the riverboat man would surely knife you in your sleep.

It seemed a hard comprehension for Long Musket. The thoughts running through his mind were visible on his face, like a novice who had bet his last dollar against a card shark and knew he was beaten. I was a skilled fighter. There was no way, in his present condition, he could defeat me – but he tried. Twisting his face into a war cry, he came at me again and again, and each time I deflected his blade and delivered a hard blow that put him on the ground. Each attack was weaker than the last, until finally, he was slow getting back onto his feet. When he paused on all fours to collect his senses, I went on the attack. I took two steps and kicked him hard in the abdomen. The force of my boot drove the wind from his lungs, and sent him rolling in the dirt gasping for air.

He was completely at my mercy. There was nothing stopping me from killing him. It would have been easy for me to bring my knife down in a plunging stroke straight through his chest, but I did not. Between breaths, Long Musket looked up at me through squinted eyes, obviously wondering why I had not yet delivered the killing blow. My delay drew anger from the other warriors.

"He has fought you like a man," Red Vest said grimly. "Do not taunt him. Give him a swift death."

"He is indeed a brave warrior," I replied. "Blood has been drawn. Honor is intact. There is no need for killing. Tell him it would bring me great sadness to send such a brave warrior to rest with his fathers before his time.

"You must kill him!" Red Vest demanded, though I could see in his eyes some inner turmoil. It clearly pained him to say it. I concluded Long Musket was either his son, or one that was dear to him.

"I do not wish to kill him," I said succinctly. "Whites without honor stole your ponies. Let me make amends for the evil they have done by giving this man his life."

The other warriors may have understood some of what I said, but they did not seem pleased with the idea. Red Vest, on the other hand, smiled at me thankfully, but still with a measure of pride. He said something to the others, and they instantly helped Long Musket to his feet and back onto his horse. The bloody and battered brave said nothing. His face was twisted with pain, but he never took his eyes off me, and I could not determine, at that time, whether he looked at me with gratefulness, or with hatred, for sparing his life.

I was to find out much later.

Red Vest knew well our customs and reached out a hand. "I take your hand in friendship today," he said. "Tomorrow, it may not be so between us. There is trouble coming. The war drums beat on the wind. We have seen the signs."

"I hope that is not the case," I said, shaking hands with him.

"A word of advice to my white friend," he said. "Do not travel these mountains alone. The evil spirits grow stronger and tempt our young men to war. A lone white is very tempting to a young brave who has not yet proven himself." He glanced once at Long Musket as if to illustrate that fact.

"Much obliged. I'll take that under consideration. Now, I have a few words of advice for you." Red Vest seemed taken aback by this, but I continued. "Don't look for your ponies anymore. You will not find them. The men who took them knew you would come looking for them – men who would be glad if the Apache and the white man went to war. Go back to your village. Let the white eyes find only the wind in these mountains."

He gave no indication that he grasped what I was saying, other than to stare hard into my eyes, as if to search my soul. Finally, he nodded and mounted his horse.

The Apaches rode away in a flurry of dust, and, before I could count to ten, there was no trace of them.

CHAPTER V   Dougson

I began my descent on the long winding road to the wooded valley floor. Carondelet was a sure-footed horse, but I took due precautions, walking alongside him, keeping myself between him and the sharp drop off on one side, while Don Carlos and Ulysses followed obediently behind, seemingly unfazed.

Things were beginning to fall into place in my mind, though many mysteries remained. The two dead horses had had me befuddled until I came upon the Apaches. No doubt, the men I had killed were the ones who had stolen the ponies from Red Vest's village. What better way to implicate the Indians in the churchmen's murders than to ensure a war party was roving the same woods at the same time?

Dougson was less than a day's ride away. I would not be surprised if the murderers had arranged for a posse to be roaming the plateau at the same time, that the Indians might be implicated, hunted down, and killed before anyone's suspicions were raised over the true events. Maybe the murderers had planned on taking news of the massacre back to Dougson, as if they had simply stumbled across the scene of the crime. If that had been the plan, then it was now left to the youth Jesse to see it through. Perhaps the lad was already in Dougson reporting his version of the events to the local sheriff.

But the question still remained, why had those churchmen been murdered?

I pondered this as the forested valley grew ever closer with each successive switchback. I was about half-way to the bottom when I saw movement in the distance – a strand of color along the dirt road winding in and out of the sea of green. I saw a long line of horses bearing blue-jacketed riders. It was a column of U.S. cavalry, riding west, the same direction I was heading. They were at least three hours ahead of me. Whether they were chasing renegade Apaches or simply on patrol, there was no way of knowing. I could not help but wonder if their presence here had somehow been pre-arranged by the murderers, hoping the soldiers would come across Red Vest's band.

A pall of smoke hung over the hills a few miles beyond the cavalry column. Beneath that smoke stood the frontier town of Dougson, where I might find answers, but I wasn't sure I wanted answers. Though I had already shot three men dead and nearly killed a fourth in a knife fight, I didn't want to be involved. The town was just a stop for me, not my final destination. I could skip it, skirt around it, and head on to the mining camps in the Verde Valley. It was only seventy or eighty miles farther. I could manage that on my few remaining provisions. If I got low, I could hunt my food easily enough. There was plenty of game along the trail. Besides, should this Jesse have made it to Dougson before me, I might find myself having to explain my actions, and I would rather not.

Bypassing the town would have been the wise thing to do. But I had no whiskey, and I really wanted a drink...

I rode into Dougson midmorning of the next day. It was a small town, situated amongst the ponderosa pines hugging the base of the Mogollon rim. It was a junction of sorts, with a handful of water mills and ranches dotting the landscape within a dozen miles. For the trappers, miners, prospectors, and ranchers that made their living in these hills, it served as a stopping-off place, a glimpse of civilization in an otherwise untamed land.

After stopping on the outskirts of Dougson to board Don Carlos and Ulysses at a place called the Johnstone Livery Stable, the first real sign of civilization I had seen in nearly two weeks, I rode on into town searching for that drink I so longed for.

Dougson's main street consisted of a collection of saloons, gunsmiths, saddleries, and general stores facing each other across a wide dirt expanse. It was frequented by only a few on this day, which I confirmed was Thursday, after checking a bulletin board displayed in a store window. Men lounged in clusters on various corners of the disjointed boardwalk. Women wearing bonnets and plain pioneer dresses walked with baskets in their arms, coming and going from the general stores. Three boys teased a dog with a stick, tossing the stick between them as the hound leaped in vain to intercept it. Laundry hung out to dry from several balconies. A smith's hammer beat out a slow rhythm far up the street. Most of the passing citizens glanced at me with suspicion but not hostility. I was a stranger to them. I had been a stranger many times before, in many other towns. The greeting here was not unlike the others, but there was something in the air, a quiet tension that had nothing to do with me. I could not quite put my finger on it. It felt like a wake, though none were dressed for mourning. Had the boy Jesse already brought word of the murders?

But all these sights and sounds meant nothing to me once I spied the open doors of the town saloon, through which wafted the gentle tune of a piano. I spurred

Carondelet toward that melody as Ulysses might have steered his galley toward the sirens and onto the rocks.

Outside the saloon, a troop of twenty or so cavalrymen in blue lounged beside their mounts, smoking and chatting, looking back at me with mild curiosity, but nothing more. They were black men, one of the units dubbed Buffalo Soldiers by the Indians. Their faces and uniforms were white with the dust of the trail, and it was clear this was the same troop I had seen from a distance the day before. Three Apaches stood a few paces away, speaking amongst themselves in their native tongue. They wore thick, red, tribal headbands, like those worn by Red Vest and his band, but these Indians also wore army blue coats. They cradled rifles in their arms and wore cartridge belts across their torsos. They were obviously scouts, given sergeant's ranks, and paid to use their unique skills in the hunting of renegades. Their severe features told of many hard campaigns. Most likely, they had served on both sides during the long series of conflicts between the U.S. Government and the Apache tribes.

I dismounted Carondelet and hitched him to the post. The sign above the awning identified the establishment as the Two Players Saloon. It was good enough. Kicking the dust off my boots, I walked up the hollow stairs, my spurs singing with each step, the smell of the liquor within drawing me to it like iron to a magnet. Entering, I found a large room filled with tables for gambling and drinking, some of which were being used, even this early in the day. A staircase to the right led up to a catwalk that wrapped around the room above the gaudy chandeliers and served as a second floor. The long bar along the opposite wall appeared to be the long trunk of a pine tree, cut in half, sanded and polished to a shine. Two upright pianos filled the far corner, one old, one new, both facing each other. A man wearing a brown, wool suit and polished, knee-high riding boots sat at the newer one. He looked to be in his mid-thirties, about my age and build, though somewhat more studious-looking, with wire-rimmed spectacles, well-groomed hair, and a handlebar mustache. A derby hat sat on the bench beside him. His getup was quite out of place on the western frontier, but would have been perfectly ordinary were this Boston or New York City. He played softly, hardly lifted his hands from the keys, his eyes closed as if he were lost in another time and another place. The opposite piano had seen better days, scarred and cracked, its upper paneling dressed with what appeared to be three bullet holes. The contrasting instruments undoubtedly fulfilled the saloon's namesake.

An army officer leaned against the bar, downing a glass of whiskey as if to savor it. He nodded kindly to me as I sidled up to the polished counter. The officer appeared much friendlier than the portly bartender who was drying a large glass with a towel, and who seemed more interested in a nearby table where two men appeared to be involved in an intense discussion. The bartender looked as though he expected a canary to burst from beneath the checkered table cloth at any moment. He turned around to set the dry glass upside down neatly on the shelf behind him with many others, and then turned back to attend me.

"What'll you have, mister?" He did not smile at me, nor did he even look at me directly, but continued to study the nearby table.

"Whiskey," I replied, setting a coin on the bar. "The whole bottle."

The bartender absent-mindedly produced the glass and a bottle, hurriedly poured the first drink for me, and then went back to drying glasses while observing the two men at the table.

I saw the officer raise his eyebrows as he stared at the bottle, whether out of shock or admiration I could not tell.

"Long patrol?" I asked, to break the silence. He was obviously as much of a visitor here as I was.

"Damnable long," he replied. "And nothing to show or it."

"I saw your men as I descended the plateau."

"Did you now?" His smile faded somewhat, and he drew a suspicious expression. "I'm not sure I caught your name, Mister..."

"Jones," I said, extending a hand.

"Major Roland Garrett, K Company, Tenth Cavalry, out of Fort Apache," he said formally, shaking my hand and then resuming his doubtful tone. "And what was your business on the reservation, Mister Jones, if you don't mind my asking?"

"No business. Just passing through."

"Coming from where?"

"Silver City." I was unsure if this officer knew anything about the murders, but something told me I had best not mention them. I smiled innocently. "I'm hauling goods, Major – luxury goods - mirrors, silks, perfumes, and a few other whimsical items, bound for the boudoirs of the lovely ladies of Prescott and the Verde Valley."

"Harrumpf!" was his only reply. I could not tell if it was out of disgust for my cargo, or to dispute my assertion that there were indeed lovely ladies in the locales referenced. He took another sip from his glass.

"What's wrong, Major? Indian trouble?"

After a long circumspect glance, he appeared to let his guard down slightly. "Yes. I'm afraid so. But it's not the Indians who are making the trouble."

"Who is then?"

"White men. There have been reports of white men on the reservation, going where they please, disturbing the natives' sacred sites. You didn't see any other white men in your travels, did you, Mister Jones?"

I thought for a moment, if I should tell him about the men that had attacked me, but then it would be hard to explain convincingly that I had left three men dead, and that I had simply killed them in self-defense.

I finally shook my head.

"Neither did we," the major replied despondently. "Sometimes I think I'm chasing ghosts. Well, I suspect it's no concern of yours. If you're headed west, Mister Jones, you shouldn't meet with any problems. There aren't any problems in the Verde Valley – at least not this week. In fact, it's quite serene across the entire territory right now. It must be, if I'm spending my time searching for grave robbers. Well," He paused to throw back the remnants of his glass, then dropped a few coins on the bar. "I wish you well on your travels and fortunes, Mister Jones."

"You, too, Major. I hope you catch them."

"Good day to you, sir."

The major left the saloon, and soon hooves clopped on the street outside as the cavalry troop departed. The tip left by the army officer went uncollected for a long time. The bartender, and nearly everyone else, for that matter, were still casting apprehensive glances at the table where the two men conversed.

One of the men at the table was verbose, with a voice that carried across the room. He was tall, broad of shoulder and girth, and wore the work clothes of a ranch hand. The other was older, perhaps in his forties, with streaks of gray above his ears. He wore an immaculate gray coat and vest that fit his trim frame perfectly.

I drank my whiskey in silence and tried to listen to what I could of their conversation.

"I got three hundred head of cattle down in Graham County, all fat from grazing along the Gila River," the larger man said, pointing to a ledger laid open on the table between them, seemingly oblivious to all but his associate. "The Mexicans will give me twenty-eight dollars a head, but I'd rather sell to an American, of course. It's my patriotic duty, you understand. I'm going to offer them to you, Mister Martinique, for twenty-six dollars a head. What do you say? Do we have a deal? That's quite a bargain, if you ask me."

Martinique, the man in the gray coat, gazed back at the haggling rancher, his aquiline features assuming a dismissive expression. Clearly, he was not impressed by the offer.

"I'm afraid that is unacceptable, Mister Thomas," Martinique replied. "We have been over this many times. You are, perhaps, having difficulty understanding? I have already told you the price I will pay. Twenty-two dollars a head, no more." Martinique had a slight accent that was not Spanish. It sounded more like that of a Frenchman I had once known on the Mississippi. Though he had the refined manner of an easterner, his tanned skin told of many years spent in the West. His voice was intelligent, quiet, and calm, the exact opposite of the man with whom he now bargained, yet somehow, I knew every word from Martinique's mouth carried poisonous daggers.

"That's plumb highway robbery!" The rancher Thomas exclaimed. "What kind of an offer is that? I've got a wife and three daughters to care for."

"I am afraid that is my final offer, Mister Thomas."

"Well, I won't do it! I tell you, I won't! The Mexicans will – "

"Then take them to Mexico," Martinique replied dismissively, waving his hand.

The rancher Thomas clearly did not appreciate the interruption. He slammed his palm down on the table. "The hell with you, Martinique! That's just what I'm gonna do!"

Thomas rose abruptly to storm out the saloon, and was half-way to the door when the Frenchman spoke again, his tone subdued, yet threatening.

"I wish you a pleasant journey, Mister Thomas. You do not need me to remind you that it is a very long way from your ranch in Graham County to Nogales – over one hundred miles across the open desert."

Thomas stopped in his tracks and turned around slowly, his fists clenched, his face showing visible restraint. "And just what might you mean by that?"

Martinique smiled with his lips and removed a cigarette from a box on the table. As if on cue, a man rose from a crowded table on the far side of the room, and I nearly choked on my whiskey. The man wore an impressive pair of pistols, one on each hip, holstered into a gun belt adorned with silver studs. His hat hung back off his head, dangling on his back from a string around his neck. He was Hispanic, with dark, tousled hair, and a wide mustache amid a face full of dark stubble. With thumbs tucked into the front of his gun belt, he sauntered over to Martinique's table, as if he had been summoned. The gunman's eyes never left those of the rancher Thomas as he took up a position just behind Martinique's chair, and a hush descended on the room as if this gunman now standing behind his boss silently communicated an impending terror. It was as if Martinique had just laid down the winning hand in a high-stakes card game, and the Frenchman wore a smug look as he struck a match and lit the cigarette between his lips.

This new chain of events had a distressing effect on Thomas, judging by the anxious expression that suddenly consumed his face.

"You know Julio, do you not, Mister Thomas?" Martinique said, casually gesturing at the gunman standing behind him. "My meaning is clear, I think. It is a dangerous country. Anything can happen. If you deal with me, I will pay you today, and will not demand any recompense should you lose a reasonable number of the herd bringing them here. Would you get such a deal from the Mexicans?"

Thomas's nervous eyes flitted around the room, most likely to see what he was up against. I saw him eye the paused card games at the other tables, then the bartender, then me, glancing once at my holstered weapon, then finally at the gunman, Julio, whose eyes had still not left him. The piano player continued to play quietly, his eyes still closed, seemingly unfazed by the increasing tension in the room, but I somehow sensed that he was paying full attention.

"I'm much obliged to you, Martinique," Thomas finally replied, somewhat amicably. "But, all the same, I'll take my business to Nogales."

The Frenchman blew out a long stream of smoke that wafted over to where Thomas was standing, several feet away. The big man turned to leave, but Martinique spoke again.

"Tell me again about your daughters, Mister Thomas. How old did you say they were? Twelve, ten, and seven, was it? They have red hair like yours, am I right? And your wife, such a lovely, plump woman. They live on your ranch, don't they? What kind of a greedy man would leave such lovely women folk all alone while he drove his herd so far south just to gain a few dollars?"

Thomas turned back to face him, his features red with anger, though when he finally spoke it was forcibly calm and collected.

"I don't take kindly to threats, Martinique. I don't take threats from any man."

"I made no threat, Mister Thomas," Martinique chuckled lightly. "I believe you are not thinking clearly."

Thomas did not smile. "I'll ask you to apologize for mentioning my women in a saloon, and for your ungentlemanly threats against their well-being."

"Or what, Thomas?"

Thomas stood up straighter. He wore a pistol, too. It was a simple Colt in an untethered holster, not that of a gunfighter. He had obviously made his way through life trusting in his size to settle most fights, but size made little different in the West. Speed, accuracy, a dead-eyed determination, an acceptance that one would either kill his opponent or have his own light snuffed out, were the keys to survival among those who made their trade with the gun. I sensed Thomas had none of these. He was a simple rancher, but now he attempted to appear more than that. He stood tall, with the ledger tucked under his left arm, and his right hand hovering dangerously close to his weapon.

Julio did not move. He stood there, blank-faced, a toothpick dangling from one lip. He appeared as calm and casual as a man watching a cow eat grass, but I saw something different, something most would not have seen. As a seasoned sailor could tell the set of a ship's rigging at a mere glance, I could read Julio. I saw the trademark signs of a cold-blooded killer, the set of the shoulders, the eyes, the hands, and a dozen other things only another gunfighter would recognize. As sure as the sun rises and sets, it was clear to me that Thomas would be dead a heartbeat after he made one move for his gun. I was uncertain whether Thomas was aware of this.

The rancher glanced around the room again, clearly undergoing an inner turmoil. Should he back down under Martinique's threat, the dozen or so witnesses would surely talk. Word of his cowardice – for that's how it would be relayed – would reach his own town, and he would become a laughing stock among friends and business associates alike.

"My quarrel is with you, Martinique," Thomas said finally, his rattled nerves evident in his voice. He pointed at Julio. "I've no beef with this young man."

Martinique glanced over his shoulder at the gunman and smiled complacently. "Ah, but it appears Julio has a beef with you, Mister Thomas. You must apologize to young Julio, I think."

"Apologize to him?" Thomas said incredulously. "What for?"

"You see, I am like a father to young Julio. It has distressed him greatly to hear such wild accusations made against me. Can't you see the pain in his eyes?"

There was nothing in Julio's eyes but the cold gaze of a killer. His face did not flinch as he stared at Thomas, as a cat might eye a wayward bird before pouncing for the kill.

"For myself, I feel no insult." Martinique continued. "It takes more than the irrational claims of a failed rancher to offend me. But I think young Julio here is not so forgiving."

"I won't do it!" Thomas exclaimed, his tone not as certain as his statement.

Martinique eyed him coldly, his smile fading. "Then perhaps you will die, Mister Thomas."

With great discomfort, I watched the indecision in Thomas's face, almost willing him not to try it, to keep his hand away from his gun. He felt insulted, that he must act to save his honor. He glanced at me again. I don't know why. But in that brief glimpse, I looked intensely into his eyes from across the room and shook my head ever so slightly, hoping he would understand and come to his senses. But my unspoken warning did not register in those nerve-shaken eyes, and they once again looked at the gunman facing him down. Thomas clearly saw no way out of his predicament. He could not retreat and save face, nor could he apologize to a man he had not wronged.

He must draw, and so he must die.

I knew he would die, because I knew the man he faced, and his name was not Julio. It was Jose Hernandez, one of the most dangerous gunfighters in the New Mexico Territory. I had recognized him from the moment he rose from the table, and wondered if he had recognized me. Several years back, Jose and I had been enemies of sorts, two gunfighters on different sides of a range war down near Las Cruces. Though he and I never squared off with each other personally, I certainly knew of his exploits, and buried many of his victims. Like all such wars, it was a dirty business, with atrocities committed by both sides. Eventually, after much useless bloodshed, the rancher Jose worked for was indicted on some ridiculous federal code violation that had nothing to do with the war, but effectively ended it all the same. With several murder charges hanging over his head, Jose – or I should say Julio now – disappeared. I never knew what became of him – until now.

From the look on Thomas's face, and that of every other man in the room, Julio had developed a similar reputation in these parts. But reputation or no, Thomas seemed foolishly intent on preserving his own honor. I am quite certain he would have gone for his gun in the next moment, and would therefore have died in the next moment, had Martinique not spoken.

"Of course, we can resolve this peacefully, Mister Thomas," the Frenchman said. "I despise bloodshed so, and poor Julio has only recently been released from the territorial prison after serving time for the last man he killed in self-defense. I propose, instead of apologizing to him, you apologize to me."

"Apologize to you?"

Martinique ignored Thomas's dumbfounded expression. "I, of course, would accept your apology for face value, but my young friend here is very hard to convince. He always needs solid proof of a man's sincerity. So, I propose you sell your herd to me, as we discussed, as a sign of your good will. Julio will see that you've made proper amends, and we can all go about our business. Then you may ride back home to those pretty girls of yours a richer man." He glanced at Julio and smiled slyly. "It would be a shame, Mister Thomas, for you and Julio to be at odds with each other. You have more in common than you know. Your daughters have auburn hair. Julio's late wife had hair of the same color. Unfortunately, he found her in the arms of another man and, in a moment of blind passion, killed them both. Ever since, he has had a peculiar penchant for red-haired women."

The intent of this new threat reverberated with Thomas, who seemed to be losing his resolve with each passing moment. Finally, the weight of the moment overcame him, and he collapsed onto the nearest chair, nodding his assent with his head in his hands.

"Very wise, Mister Thomas," Martinique said, dousing his cigarette, then rising and offering a hand.

Thomas took it, shook it half-heartedly, then pushed it away as if it were leprous. Slouching, his face now ashen, he looked like a man who had been dragged through the streets and who had lost every last ounce of self-respect.

Martinique, on the other hand, was bright and cheerful. He placed a hand on the big man's slumping shoulders. "Come now, Thomas. Be happy. I'm sure after you've had some time to think it over, you'll realize you made the right decision." He gestured to the door. "Walk with me now to the clerk's office, and we'll draw up the contract and see you on your way, back to that lovely family of yours."

The sullen rancher looked as though he would never forgive himself for backing down, but he did as Martinique said, and the two walked out the door together. At the same time, a retinue of gunmen rose from the same table at which Julio had been sitting before, and followed them out. Evidently, they were Martinique's entourage and bodyguard.

Julio was the last to leave, but, before he passed through the swinging doors, he looked over his shoulder directly at me. It was just a brief glance, but the recognition was there.

Once you decide to make your living with the gun, you can never turn back, you can never walk away. Not because you long for such a life, but because it never lets you escape. You try to elude it, try to deny the violent code you once lived by, but it is always there, creeping after you like a demon intent on possessing your soul.

I never should have come here.

CHAPTER VI   Just Passin' Through

My mother always told me the drink would be my undoing. My desire to satiate my thirst had led me to foolish decisions before, and I suppose the lessons of the past had never quite sunk in.

As a dog returns to his vomit, so shall a fool return to his folly.

She liked quoting that proverb, bless her soul.

As the saloon doors flapped shut, the whole room seemed to breathe easier, including the bartender who now smiled at me as if I had just arrived and had not been standing there for the better part of a quarter hour. As if a fog bank had suddenly lifted, the mood transformed to a lazy, casual environment.

"Can I get you anything else, mister?" the barkeep asked politely. "Something to eat, maybe?"

"No, thanks."

The two tables populated by active card games got back into full swing. A few of the players afforded brief glances away from their hands to look my way. One fellow wearing a checkered shirt looked a little longer than the others. I turned my attention away, cursing inwardly, and wondering if his memory was as good as mine. I also wondered just how much of a fool I was. If Jose – I mean, Julio – was here, then I should have expected others from his bunch to be here as well. The man in the checkered shirt, for instance.

"Passing through?" asked the bartender.

I nodded.

"We don't see too many strangers around here," he continued. "Not since they finished the railroad through Flagstaff, earlier this year. Where did you say you were from, mister?"

I hadn't said, but the bartender had asked the probing question loud enough for most of the others in the room to hear, as if it were his job to satisfy their curiosity. If my answers were not as loud and as strong, they would all think I was rude, or I had something to hide. Unfortunately, I was, and I did.

"Albuquerque," I answered simply, but not entirely truthfully. I had been to Albuquerque, just not in over a year.

His eyes darted to the revolver holstered at my belt, as if he had just noticed it.

"What was your business there, if you don't mind my asking?" His tone was more inquisitive than friendly.

When I did not answer, but simply took another drink, he glanced at my gun again.

"That's a might fancy sidearm you're wearing, mister." His eyes cut nervously from me to the others in the room, as if to ensure there were plenty of men around to assist him in throwing me out, if the need arose. "You wouldn't have come here looking for trouble, would you?"

Now he was just being a nuisance. I had not hardly drained my second glass, and felt like I was on the witness stand. Could a man not enjoy a glass of whiskey without having to answer for his comings and goings?

I took a silver dollar from my shirt pocket and set it on the bar.

"Come to think of it," I said. "There is something I'd like."

"Yes, sir." He eyed the coin as if he wanted to reach out and grab it. "Of course. Anything you like."

"I'd like you to shut up and mind your own business! I want ten minutes without your fat face filling my ears with words. During that time, I'm going to drink my whiskey. Then I'm going to walk out that door and leave this dung heap of a town behind me, and none of these things you want to know are really going to matter. If you can do that for ten minutes, there's another dollar in it for you. Can you do that?"

It was, perhaps, not the best choice of words, but after seeing Jose Hernandez for the first time in four years, and now, with the man in the checkered shirt still eyeing me from across the room, I was frustrated, more with myself, than with anything else. For my own longing for the drink had put me in this predicament.

The bartender was clearly offended by my tirade, but nodded submissively and drifted farther down the bar, taking a handful of newly washed glasses with him to dry.

Across the room, the piano player began a new tune. I noticed he was looking in my direction. He smiled at me in a friendly manner, as if in greeting, and then went back to his musical trance.

Now that I was alone, I tried to relax. Under the mind-numbing influence of the strong liquor, I tried to purge from my memory the faces of the men I had killed up on the plateau. That was why I was here, after all. I had killed three men – one, arguably, in cold blood. The killer within me, that beast I had managed to subdue for so long, had shown its ugly head once again. I wanted to drink the whole bottle, to get falling-down drunk, and wake up in some whore's bed, not because I had killed those men – but because I had enjoyed it.

But I could not relax. The gunfighter in me felt the eyes boring a hole through my back. I knew the man in the checkered shirt was watching my every move, but I did not turn to look at him.

Ten minutes passed and nothing happened. The bartender, recovered from the upbraiding, approached me again. Any frontier businessman could not resist the opportunity of tapping his few patrons for as much money as possible, no matter how rude those patrons were.

"Anything else I can get you, mister?" he asked with some hesitation.

I shook my head.

"You have my apologies, sir," he said shamefacedly. "We don't get many visitors around here. Now, it seems there's a flood of them." He cut his eyes at the piano player, and then back at me. "Won't you stay the night? We have rooms available."

"Like I said, I'm just passing through."

"Suit yourself, mister."

He started to move away again, but then a thought entered my head, something that had been niggling at the back of my mind, a curiosity that had to be satisfied. Six churchmen had been murdered up on the plateau, six men who were, by all appearances, no threat to anyone. I wanted to know why they had died.

I wanted to know more than was good for me.

"There is one thing," I said, stopping him. "*San Miguel*. Does that name mean anything to you?"

His smile faded. Again, he glanced in the direction of the piano player who still seemed oblivious to all but his music. The bartender's demeanor was suddenly almost as nervous as it had been during the showdown between Martinique and Thomas. When he spoke again, he did so quietly, such that none of the others in the room could hear.

"I suppose it means something to folks around here, mister. Seems to be of interest to many of our guests lately, too. What do you want to know about it?"

"What is it?"

"It's an old Spanish mission a few miles outside of town." He eyed me suspiciously. "Mind if I ask what business you have there?"

"No business," I said innocently. I should have stopped there, but the mention of the mission clearly made the bartender uncomfortable, so I decided to see how much he knew. "A couple nights back, I shared a campfire with some churchmen on the trail. They mentioned that name several times."

The bartender looked at me as though I had just told him the sky was purple. He seemed much disturbed by the revelation.

"You say you spoke to them?" he asked skeptically.

I nodded and took another drink, trying to maintain the lie as best as I could. I was testing him, and it seemed to me that he knew precisely of whom I spoke.

"Churchmen?" He ventured carefully, as if he did not want to ask more but was compelled to. "You mean priests?"

"I supposed they could have been. They never told me who they were. It was dark when I entered their camp, and dark the next morning when I took my leave of them. Polite fellas, though."

"You say two nights ago?"

I nodded again. "They were headed east. I figured they had to come from somewhere nearby. I offered payment for their hospitality, but they wouldn't accept it. I can't abide being in debt to a man, so I thought I'd try to find somewhere I could leave some token of gratitude for their troubles. If San Miguel is a church, all the better."

The bartender laughed nervously. "A church? There's not much there but a few crumbling walls and a bell tower. Not too many Catholics around here these days."

"Is the mission still in use? Are priests still there?"

He nodded. "Up until a few days ago. They all packed up and left." Again, the bartender appeared astonished, as if still digesting this news.

"Well, then, I suppose it had to be them." I shrugged. "Unless some other large party passed through here recently, heading in the same direction."

He shook his head, glancing anxiously at the card games on the other side of the room.

"Well," I said, placing the glass on the bar firmly to indicate I had downed my last shot. "That's good news. Now I know where to take this." I pulled out the wooden cross I had kept in my jacket, and placed it next to the empty glass.

The bartender's eyes bulged out as he gazed upon it, like I had just thrown a piece of raw meat onto the bar.

"The mission's nearby, you say?" I asked, intrigued by his reaction.

He nodded, still staring at the cross, almost in a trancelike state. "Eight miles south of here. Now that the priests have left, it's all but deserted. I expect there's no one there but the groundskeeper, now." The bartender spoke mechanically, as if troubled over some decision he must make. Finally, he put away the glass he had been drying and produced a fresh bottle of whiskey, setting it on the table before me.

"Why leave so soon, mister?" he said awkwardly, filling my glass again. "Have a cigar, and a drink on the house, and feel free to fill yourself another. I must step out for a few minutes, but I will return shortly. Please don't leave yet."

He made his way around the bar and headed for the door, walking quickly, like a man holding a stick of dynamite with a lit fuse. I downed the drink in one shot and allowed him to get to the door before calling after him.

"Barkeeper!"

He stopped in his tracks, and turned his head, the temptation to keep walking evident on his face. The recollection of my holstered six-gun had surely convinced him to do otherwise.

"Yes, mister?" he said.

"The cross. I'll take that."

His face broke into a shameful grin as if he had forgotten it was in his hand.

"Of course," he said, sauntering over to return it to me. "How absent-minded of me. Here you are."

He watched me place it back inside my coat as a cowboy might watch a dancing girl's cleavage after a six-week cattle drive. Then, without another word, he left the saloon, walking briskly. I did not know where he was going, clearly to tell someone about the cross and my far-fetched story, but something told me I didn't want to be around when he returned.

I downed the rest of the glass, took my bottle, and headed for the door, distracted briefly by the piano player, who had begun to strike the wrong keys for the first time since I had entered the room. Looking up, I discovered the reason why. The man in the checkered shirt was at the door, standing in my path. His face was grim, and he eyed me with a baleful stare.

His name was Frank Garfield – an old acquaintance of mine, for lack of a better term. His hands were on his hips, and that was a good thing for him, because now I would let him live. Any other stance would have changed my response to him.

He must have expected me to stop and face him, but I did not. I took two quick steps and laid a solid fist to his jaw. The blow took him completely by surprise. He fell backward out the saloon doors, onto the platform and the steps beyond. A woman across the street screamed as he tumbled down into the street, drawing the attention of several passers-by.

Ignoring them all, I did not stop but kept walking to my horse. I had begun to loose Carondelet's reins when a voice filled with loathing and hatred spoke behind me.

"Turn around, you murderer! Turn around, damn you, and face me like a man!"

I did not turn around, at first. I knew Frank had gotten to his feet, shamed and now consumed with an anger beyond rationality.

"Go back to your card game, Frank," I said, keeping my back to him. "Go back, have a drink, and forget you ever saw me."

"Forget the man who murdered my brother?" His voice trembled with rage. "You will face me, damn it! Turn around!"

After a long sigh, I did turn around, but only partially, not letting go of Carondelet's reins. I kept my hands away from my gun, hoping some sense would enter the fool's head. Frank stood about fifteen paces away, covered in the dust of the street, hair disheveled, bleeding from the lip, gun hand trembling as it hovered over his holster.

Maybe I should not have hit him. I had been angry about the bartender's behavior, about the events of the past few days, about running into Jose "Julio" Hernandez – and mostly about not being allowed to enjoy my whiskey in peace.

No, I probably should not have punched him. He was right, after all. I did kill his brother.

Frank Garfield, the man now facing me in the street, was the brother of Byron Garfield, an impetuous youth who thought he would try his hand at gun play. Byron thought he was fast. He thought he was good with the gun, but he wasn't. Like so many boys who enter this trade, believing themselves immortal, their eyes set on glory and fame, Byron Garfield ended up six feet under in a pinewood box long before he could mature into a rational man. And I'm the one who put him there.

People still say a lot of things about that cold, winter day, years ago, on the streets of Las Cruces – some people who weren't even there. Most who were there were Byron's misguided friends, the same ones who were largely responsible for his death. After the incident, they took to spreading lies and rumors – their own version of the events – and none of them were true. They claimed Byron was drunk, that I took advantage of him in his inebriated state, that I drew on him as he came out of a dry goods store while his hands were full. But those stories are all lies.

The truth is, Byron's friends had inflated his ego. They had heaped praises on him, marveling at his speed, telling him he could beat any man alive. When they heard I was in town, they persuaded him to seek me out, convincing him there was no better way to kick off his career than by taking down a renowned man of the trade. He met me on the street, quite by accident, and went for his gun before I could even get a word out.

We both drew, and I was quicker. That's all there was to it. I didn't shoot him in the back, as some have said. I put a bullet between his eyes at thirty paces, and he was dead before his body hit the ground.

An irrational gunman will soon be a dead gunman. Byron was irrational, and it got him killed. A professional gunman, like Julio – like me – never went seeking glory. A professional gunman never allowed himself to be driven by impulses. Julio had seen me, just as Frank had. He had recognized me, but he had just kept walking. Professional gunmen don't go looking for a fight unless they have a stake in it. Professional gunmen know the odds will someday play against them.

Frank Garfield was much like his brother, hotheaded and irrational.

Now, as Frank squared off with me, his stance clearly communicating his intent to not leave this street until one of us was dead, a hush descended on our surroundings. The nearby citizens had stopped whatever they were doing to observe the new spectacle. Men and women cleared away from the fields of fire, some pensive and anxious, some grinning with evil delight, others merely curious. Some men shielded their wives behind them as they waited for the explosive moment.

Farther down the street, in the distance beyond Frank's left shoulder, I saw Martinique and his gunmen standing on the boardwalk outside a building adorned with a swinging sign that read *Martinique, Attorney at Law*. At that moment, I had the wherewithal to consider how strange it was that this strongman rancher baron Martinique should be some squirrelly lawyer. The portly bartender was there, too, still in his white apron, whispering into Martinique's ear as both stared in my direction. I picked Julio out of the bunch, not smiling, not frowning either, simply observing with mild professional interest.

"Drop those reins and face me like a man, damn it!" Frank spat, still shaking with anger.

By now the saloon had emptied, and all who had previously been playing cards now lined the porch. Frank would have to save face in front of his peers. I noticed the piano player standing there, too, now wearing the derby hat. Unlike the others, he did not appear excited by the prospect of a duel. Instead, he eyed me with a guarded expression, as one who contemplated interfering in an affair that was none of his business.

It was clear to me there was only one course of action. The determined look in Frank's eyes was the same one I had seen in many other men. He would not waver from his vengeance, but I felt obligated to at least try to head off the unstoppable swirl I had carelessly set in motion.

"I'm sorry about your brother, Frank. If I could have done it another way, I would have."

"You shot him in cold blood, you blackguard!" Frank said, practically hysterical. He had clearly not expected to encounter me today, and all the pain of the past was coming back to him in full force.

"You weren't there, Frank. Whatever you heard, isn't true. They lied to you. Byron drew on me, unprovoked."

"You're a liar!" he shouted. "A lily-livered liar and a back shooter!"

The reins fell from my hands, and I turned to face him squarely. After all, there was only so much a man could take. Calling a man a liar in this country was tantamount to insulting his mother, and every mother before her. Calling him yellow was an unpardonable sin.

"I won't shoot you in the back, Frank. If you don't walk away right now, you'll get it, just like your brother did."

For the first time, I saw a change in Frank's eyes, some measure of reflection crossing his face, his bravado, or the effects of the alcohol, diminishing. Now that I was facing him, now that he saw my cold, unblinking eyes, my rock-steady hand hovering inches from my holster, he was having second thoughts. He glanced once at his friends lining the porch, and I could read his thoughts as clearly as a book. He wanted to leave. He wanted to back down and take back all he had said, but he could not - not without losing face in front of all these people.

Pride goeth before destruction.

My mother liked to say that one, too.

As I watched Frank, each new thought crossing his mind reflected on his face, I witnessed the same stages of indecision I had seen so many times in the amateur opponents of my past duels. First fear, then shame, then resolve, then pride, and finally determination. In the end, only the cowards ran away, and that was unfortunate, because they were the ones who lived. I knew enough about Frank to know he was not a coward, and so he must draw. It was only a matter of time. Lucky for him, he took long enough to come to that conclusion that I had time to make a few decisions of my own.

Finally, his hand went haphazardly for his weapon, fumbling for half a heartbeat, ages in a duel. My gun was in my hand and had fired before his gun barrel had cleared the leather, the cacophony echoing in the confined street. His checkered shirt rippled near the top of his right shoulder, a splash of blood sprinkling his face and the air. He instinctively squeezed the trigger, discharging his weapon into the ground in a slew of white smoke. Then the gun fell from his hand, and he wavered on his feet, his eyes showing puzzlement and confusion, clearly aware that he had been hit, but uncertain how severely. At last, his wobbly knees gave out, probably more from fear than anything else, and he sat down in the street exactly where he had stood.

I had already holstered my weapon, and was cinching up my saddle, for I knew the wound my bullet had left in the fleshy part of his shoulder was not mortal. Unlike his unfortunate brother, I had had time to think about where I wanted to place this bullet, and it had gone precisely where I had willed it to go. Frank had preserved his honor. He would recover, and if he knew what was good for him, get out of the revenge business and let go of his brother's death.

Several of his friends, sensing the fight was over, rushed to his aid, gathering around him. I placed one boot in the stirrup to mount my horse, but was stopped short by a high-pitched voice behind me.

"Just hold it right there, mister."

I turned to see a short, round-faced man with gray hair protruding from beneath a top hat. He wore a black coat with tails one size too small for him. On one lapel, a badge identified him as Dougson's version of a lawman. He looked more like a clerk to me. He was not intimidating in the least – that is, if you took away the double-barreled shotgun he now held leveled at my mid-section.

"Climb down off that horse, mister," he said.

I complied. I had no choice.

"He drew first," I explained, gesturing at Frank.

"That's not what I saw," one of Frank's friends spoke up, marching over to stand beside the lawman. "Arrest him, sheriff. This man gunned down Frank here for no reason at all. He killed Frank's brother awhile back, and he intended to do the same to Frank."

"That's not what happened – " I started, but the lawman interrupted me.

"Shut up, mister!" He brought the shotgun to his shoulder, eyeing me down both barrels. "Now, before you do any talking, you're going to hand over that sidearm there, and then you're going to march yourself right over to my jail." He gestured to a building down the street. "Then you can talk all you want."

"Let's string him up, sheriff," said another of Frank's friends. "We don't need his kind around here."

This sentiment was echoed by the other men from the saloon who quickly gathered around to back him up, all but the piano player, who still eyed me from the porch from behind his wire spectacles. He was clearly not a part of this quickly forming lynch mob.

As the dozen or so men began clamoring for my immediate execution, while the sheriff held the gun on me and the rest of the townsfolk looked on, I saw Martinique behind the crowd. The gray-haired Frenchman stood there, calmly observing the commotion, the bartender still beside him. I saw the sheriff look to Martinique as a slave might look to a master for guidance. At a slight shake of the Frenchman's head, the sheriff raised his high-pitched voice to address the maddened crowd.

"There'll be no hanging!" he announced. "Leastwise, not until we've gotten to the bottom of this, and then only by due process of the law." He then turned back to me, and spoke sternly. "Now, mister, I'm not going to ask you again. Hand over that gun!"

This was absurd. I had only been in this town for the better part of an hour, and already I had punched and shot a man, had become the target of a mob, and was now about to be hauled off to some jail, run by who knows who, presumably the rancher-baron Martinique and his puppet sheriff.

I never should have come here.

"I'm riding out of here!" I announced to them all, hoping the display of my gunmanship was enough to give them pause, and that this sheriff didn't have an itchy trigger finger.

Turning my back on them, I reached for the pommel of my saddle, but was instantly waylaid from behind. I felt the stock of a gun, probably the shotgun, across the back of my head. It was a feeble strike, but hard enough to make me see stars. Then I was on the ground, being kicked and stomped on by boots. Through one kick to the ribs after another, I did the best I could to remain in the fetal position and keep them from getting to anything vital. Drawing my weapon on this mob would only ensure my immediate lynching, and so I did not go for it. Then one of them kicked dust into my eyes, blinding me, and preventing me from seeing whose probing hands were depriving me of all my possessions. I was helpless as my gun, my knife, my belt were all taken from me. Then another hand, this one a bit less violent than the others, reached inside my coat as if to find something its owner knew was there. At first, I thought some opportunist in the crowd was simply robbing me of the money I kept clipped inside my shirt pocket, but then I realized the hand had ignored the money clip entirely and had made off with the wooden cross. I did not see who had taken it, but I had my suspicions. The bartender had tried to make off with it before. It would have been nothing for him to grope his way through the crowd and take it, and I assumed that's what had happened.

I began cursing the crowd as the beating continued, and then cursing the sheriff for not stopping it. But my curses were cut short, when the stock of the weapon struck me across the head again, a much harder blow this time, and I lost all consciousness.

CHAPTER VII   Maha-neek

"Are you awake, Mister Jones?"

A voice called me back to the world of the living. I opened my eyes to see a low ceiling with rafters above me. My head throbbed painfully, the only relief offered by the coolness of a damp cloth placed across my forehead. My first thought was that I was in danger, that my attackers had only paused and would be on me again at any moment. I abruptly sat up on the small cot, then instantly regretted it, for it only made my head hurt worse. I closed my eyes again.

"I would advise you to lie back down, Mister Jones," the voice said. This time I detected the French accent. "The doctor has said rest is the best thing for you."

Forcing my eyes open again, I withstood the pain to examine my surroundings a bit more thoroughly. I sat in a small jail cell, hardly larger than the cot on which I lay. It had no windows, and contained nothing but the cot, a bucket, and a small wash basin. Opposite the cell, on the other side of the room, a window let in the light of the setting sun, bathing the walls of my confined chamber in a yellow light streaked with the long shadows of the bars.

I had been out for hours.

Three men stared back at me from the other side of the bars. The closest was Martinique. He sat on a stool wearing an amiable smile. Behind his right shoulder, stood the gunman Julio, eyeing me with something between pity and revulsion. Behind Martinique's left shoulder stood a young man, more like a boy, who could have been no more than sixteen. The boy looked back at me with angry, yet fearful eyes. I did not recognize him at first, until I noticed the slouch hat he held in his hands. I could pick out that wide-brimmed, oil-stained hat in a crowded market on a Sunday. This was Jesse, the same lad who had gotten away in the forest, who had ridden like blue blazes after I had shot his three Indian-disguised comrades.

So, I surmised, Martinique had something to do with those murders up there on the plateau, and this boy had likely told him everything about my chance involvement in the matter. If that was indeed the case, then why was Martinique striking such a friendly tone? And why the hell was he smiling?

Behind my three visitors, further back in the room, the sheriff sat at a desk, leaning back with his feet up on it. He smoked a cigarette while reading a newspaper folded in half on his lap, and seemed to have little interest in the visitation. On the wall behind him was a rack filled with rifles, and the shotgun that he had held on me earlier. A few gun belts, with holstered weapons, hung from pegs next to the rack. One of the belts was mine, my cherished pistol still in its holster. I could at least give this sheriff credit for being thorough, having made sure my personal belongings were retrieved from the mob.

I stared at my weapon with covetous eyes, like gazing upon one of my vital organs, surgically removed from my body and placed in a glass jar on the opposite side of the room. The Peacemaker had only left my side on a handful of occasions, and I always felt empty without it.

"You are quite an interesting man, Mister Jones," Martinique said. He gestured to the boy. "Jesse, here, tells me you killed three of my men up on the plateau. Is that true?"

I looked back at him but did not answer.

He shrugged. "And now you are caught gunning down a half-mad drunk on the streets of Dougson. An interesting man, indeed."

I was waiting for him to say that Julio had also told him I was once a hired gun down near the border in the New

Mexico Territory, but he did not. Perhaps Julio had kept our previous association to himself.

"Allow me to introduce myself, Mister Jones. My name is Pierre Martinique. Perhaps, you have heard of me?" When I did not answer, he continued unfazed. "I am a powerful man in these parts, Mister Jones. Very little transpires here without me knowing about it. For instance, if someone were to arrive in town in possession of, say, a certain token of the church, I would be the first to hear of it."

He was, no doubt, referring to the wooden cross. Surely the bartender had told him about it. That was not surprising. Nor was it surprising that Martinique was responsible for the priests' murders. The blatant extortion of the cattleman Thomas had already told me volumes about the Frenchman's character, and the lengths he was willing to go to get his way.

Clearly, Martinique's reach spread far and wide, and it suddenly occurred to me that this powerful rancher-baron was, no doubt, the man *"Maha-neek"* whom Red Vest had spoken of with trepidation.

"You're facing some serious charges, Mister Jones," he continued. "The murder of three men. The attempted murder of another. The district court will be in session in two weeks, isn't that right, Hobson?" This prompted a nod from the sheriff, who just as quickly went back to reading his paper. "Judge Masterson also happens to be a good friend of mine. It will be an open and shut case, I think, especially with Jesse's testimony. You will be hanged inside of three weeks, Mister Jones. Or, perhaps, sooner. The men you killed had many friends around here. They may decide to take the law into their own hands. I doubt if our good sheriff will be able to stop them." Hobson nodded in the background, not looking up from the paper. "So far, I have asked Jesse, here, to keep quiet about their deaths. Otherwise, I'm sure you would be swinging within the hour."

"Have you asked Jesse to keep quiet about the other murders, too?" I asked in a challenging tone. "The ones he had a hand in?" I raised my voice to make sure the sheriff heard every word. "Maybe if little Jesse, here, told the truth about how his friends died, the judge would see things differently. Maybe if Jesse told about the unarmed priests he and his partners tortured and murdered up on the rim, the judge would be more interested in Jesse than in me." I paused and looked Martinique in the eyes. "Maybe he'd be interested in you, too."

The Frenchman looked over his shoulder at the sheriff. Both exchanged glances and then laughed out loud. It was immediately clear to me I would find no ally in Sheriff Hobson. By all appearances, the sheriff was an accepting, if not willing, accomplice to this rancher strongman.

"Do you know what you are talking about, Mister Jones?" Martinique asked.

"I know that someone wanted a bunch of priests dead. I believe that someone is you. That you had little Jesse and his friends dress up like Indians and waylay the poor churchmen on the trail, making it look like Apaches had done it. That you had them steal some ponies from a nearby Apache village, hoping the Indian search party would get caught snooping around the murder scene by the troop of cavalry you arranged to have patrolling the area at the same time. Did I miss anything?"

After a few moments, in which he stared back at me, clearly not having expected me to have pieced together as much as I had, Martinique's face formed into a smile that seemed more forced than before. "But why would I do such a dreadful thing, Mister Jones?"

I shrugged, though, in truth, I was beginning to have some notion as to the reason. The thing that puzzled me more was why Martinique felt compelled to interrogate me.

If the district judge really was in his hip pocket, just as the sheriff was – and everyone else in this town, it seemed, right down to the bartender – then it really didn't matter what I thought, or what conclusions I had drawn. As he said, the case would be open and shut, and I was as good as dead. My knowledge of the priests' murders would die with me.

"Who knows?" I finally answered. "Maybe the same reason you threatened that rancher, Mister Thomas. Maybe the priests were a threat to you."

"An interesting idea, Mister Jones, but not very original," Martinique said, shaking his head.

"Maybe the judge will think otherwise."

"But who can trust the word of such a dangerous man as you – a man who has left a trail of blood and death across the territory?" Martinique then leaned in close to the bars, his face suddenly sincere. "But such men are useful to me, Jones. From what I observed in the street today, you are worth as many as five men. I need good men – good men who will take direction and carry out orders without distraction. If I had good men working for me, neither you nor I would be in the situation we now find ourselves." He cast an annoyed look at Jesse, who seemed to diminish under his stare. "I offer good money, and protection from the law for any act you perform under my employ."

When I did not reply, Martinique added. "You are an ambitious man, Jones, as I am. Men like us do not act for no reason. I sense you know more about this business than you are letting on. Otherwise, you would not have shown the cross in the saloon. If you do not wish to work for me, then perhaps you desire some kind of compensation?"

"Compensation?" I asked bewilderedly.

"Yes. How much money do you want to tell me where you have hidden the cross?"

At that moment, I realized Martinique did not have the cross. I had only assumed it had been one of his henchmen that had lifted it off me during the scuffle. Seeing as how the sheriff had gone to the trouble of recovering my gun, I could only assume they had already rifled both my person and my saddlebags for the cross not realizing it had been taken from me by someone in the mob.

With this revelation, I began to form a picture in my mind, a connected series of events, that somewhat explained how I had ended up in this jail cell with this rancher-baron, whom I had only just met, making me offers of employment and cash.

It went something like this...

I happen upon the scene of the murders in the forest while Jesse and his three cohorts are still staging the area to look like an Indian attack. They scramble away and remain out of sight while I examine the area. Purely by chance, I find the cross, the one item they had been instructed by Martinique to recover. Once I have moved on, Jesse and his friends search the area and realize I must have it. They start to follow me, indecisive about their next move. When I divert off the trail, they know they must act. They attack me. I kill all but Jesse, who high tails it for Dougson to tell Martinique the whole story. Days later, when the bartender informs Martinique I'm in the saloon, brandishing the sought-after cross, Martinique concludes I want to make a deal with him.

The Frenchman rancher did not give two hoots in hell I had killed three of his men. Neither did he care that I had wounded Frank Garfield. He only wanted that cross. It was an item for which he had already committed murder, and I got the feeling he would have no compunctions about committing several more to get his hands on it.

He was offering me my freedom, and probably anything else I desired, if only I would tell him where it was. Presumably, he thought I had hidden it shortly after showing it to the bartender. He thought I knew where it was. Something told me, that was the only reason I was still alive. Had I known where it was, I would have been happy to trade the thing, though I doubted that would have been enough to gain my freedom.

You see, up until this point, the cross had been in my possession for going on two days, and, in that time, I had discovered a few things. I was not entirely ignorant of Martinique's scheme. Yes, at that moment, sitting in that jail cell, I was in the dark as to the cross's whereabouts – but I knew precisely why Martinique wanted it.

"Money's no good to a man when he's condemned to hang," I said disdainfully to Martinique. I avoided Julio's eyes, knowing full well a professional gunman like him would be watching mine, looking for any sign of deceit.

"I think I have made it clear, I can arrange to have you released," Martinique said impatiently.

"Not that I don't trust you, Mister Martinique, but I want a little more assurance than that. You tell that sheriff of yours to release me, to drop all charges, give me back my gun, my horse, all my things, and to let me ride out of here, and I'll tell you where it is."

All four men began to laugh, Martinique and the sheriff the most fervently. Julio merely bared a row of yellow teeth, while Jesse's eyes constantly cut to the face of his boss, as if to be sure it was okay for him to laugh, too.

"Just like that, huh?" Martinique chortled.

"That's not all," I said firmly.

This silenced all four of them, but they still eyed me with amusement.

"I want a hundred dollars cash for my troubles," I continued. "Give me that, and let little Jesse ride out of town with me unarmed. Once we're far enough out, and I'm convinced we haven't been followed, I'll tell this runt where I've hidden the cross, and he can ride back to town and tell you. I'll forget all I saw up on the plateau and be on my way, a happier and richer man, and you'll have what you want. Do we have a deal?"

A hush descended on the room. None of them were smiling now, probably because Martinique's formerly genial manner had been replaced with a dark and brooding expression. Whereas before, the Frenchman had looked on me welcomingly as one he wished to hire, he now glared at me loathingly, as if he had never intended to part with any money in the first place and I had just headed off his planned deceit with my proposition.

"Men do not dictate terms to me, Jones," he said contemptuously. "They bend to my will, just as Thomas did. I found his weakness. Every man has a past. Every man has attachments. Be it some two-bit whore in Silver City, or some frail, old mother living in the East, I will find yours. Until then, you will stay where you are, and you will ponder the future. Each day brings you closer to the hangman's noose. Each day brings me closer to finding your weakness – and I will find it, Jones. I have friends in many places. The telegraph travels swiftly."

After a long moment in which he seemed to expect me to make some sort of counter-offer out of panic, he rose and walked over to the sheriff's desk.

"I must spend a few days at the ranch," Martinique said to Hobson. "If he decides to talk, or the men searching the saloon find it, send for me."

"Yes, sir, Mister Martinique," the sheriff replied obediently. "If they find anything, I'll be sure to let you know."

After a final glance in my direction, Martinique left the jailhouse, followed by Jesse. Julio, however, lingered behind, approaching the bars to my cell and looking down at me, his eyes studying me as a sculptor might gaze upon a rival's handiwork.

"It has been a long time, amigo," he said finally.

"Not long enough," I replied unenthusiastically.

A measure of gloominess crossed his face. "I am sad you are in jail, amigo. I would be even sadder should you hang."

I met his eyes and fully understood his meaning. During those days in Las Cruces, though our paths never crossed in a gunfight, we well knew of each other's existence. We both knew we were the top guns on each side. As I said before, a professional gunfighter does not go looking for a fight unless he has a stake in it, but he is always curious – curious as to who will be the one to best him, for very few of us live to old age. And right now, Julio gazed upon me with curiosity. There was something niggling at the back of his thoughts, a nagging question that had probably resurfaced when he first saw me in the saloon a few hours ago.

Which of us was faster?

With a slight nod, Julio turned on his heel and strode out of the jail, the clink of his spurs fading outside. A heavy silence fell on the room as I was left alone with Sheriff Hobson.

The bars of my cell and a few feet were all that stood between us, but it was no use. The cell looked to be of sound construction. There was no way I could escape, and a chalk line drawn on the floor boards a few feet from my cell told me the sheriff was wary of venturing too close to the bars of an occupied cell.

Hobson met eyes with me from across the room, as if he were reading my thoughts. Then, with a smug smile, he leaned back in his chair and went back to reading his paper.

CHAPTER VIII   The Piano Player

Night fell on the town of Dougson, my only perception of it the fading light in the window opposite my cell. Hobson stepped out at sunset, leaving me alone to stare at my gun across the room, and listen to the sounds of merriment coming from the nearby saloons. Boots thumped on the boardwalk outside as the town's evening foot traffic strolled past the jail house. Each time I heard more than a few footfalls, I wondered if Hobson had decided to turn me over to the lynch mob. But eventually, he returned, wreaking of alcohol and of a dinner that had clearly contained a liberal serving of onions.

"Here," he said unceremoniously, as he used a broomstick to shove a tin slopping with some kind of stew through a slot near the bottom of the bars. "Eat it fast, and pass me back the plate."

I had not eaten all day, and was too hungry to care what it was. I quickly scarfed it all down with the small wooden spoon provided, complying more with the pangs of my stomach than with Hobson's orders.

The sheriff watched me with revulsion, as one might observe a wild animal tear into a fresh kill. When I was finished, he took the plate, tossed it onto a table, then propped open the window and began to smoke, belching and passing gas as freely as if he were alone. I considered striking up a conversation with him, to see if there was some aspect of Hobson that might be inclined to let me go. It was clear to me he was a puppet, that his position, his status, his livelihood depended on him staying in the good graces of Martinique, but maybe there was some angle I could take with him. No matter what the organization was, be it the crew of a riverboat, a mining camp, or a criminal gang, the hired help always had their grievances. Maybe I could play on one of these.

I was about to say something, when there was a knock on the door. The door opened, and a mustached man wearing a brown suit, derby hat, and spectacles walked in. I was shocked when I realized it was the piano player from the saloon.

He glanced once in my direction, then removed his derby hat and nodded to the sheriff. "Good evening, sheriff."

Hobson looked back at him quizzically, as if he had never seen the man before, and I immediately deduced they must not have met because the piano player extended a hand.

"My name is Quinn. Allen Quinn."

Quinn's voice carried a distinct northeastern accent.

"Evening, Mister Quinn," Hobson replied warily. "Glad to meet you. You're that fella I saw over at the saloon this morning, banging out a tune. Leastways, I guess that's what you call it."

Though appearing somewhat offended, Quinn did not let his annoyance carryover into his tone. "Yes, well, the owner of the establishment was kind enough to let me play. I find it relaxing. It was *Oh, Dry the Glist'ning Tear* from *The Pirates of Penzance*, a piece they're playing in New York City now. I don't suppose you've heard it before."

"Can't say that I have," Hobson replied brusquely, as if he had no desire to ever hear it again. "I hear you've been asking a lot of questions around town."

"Around town?" Quinn said cocking his head to one side. "No, I don't think so, sheriff. Just making casual conversation. I've spoken to the bartender across the street, and a few of the patrons. That's all. Not a very talkative bunch, and somewhat dull-witted, in my humble opinion."

Hobson gazed at Quinn with suspicious eyes. Clearly, he had not yet gotten around to checking out this newcomer from the East. "People around here don't like strangers poking their noses into their business."

"Who does, sheriff? I suppose even the dregs of humanity have their fancies."

This last was said somewhat condescendingly, and I could see it rankled Hobson. Folk in the West had a presupposition about anyone who dressed and acted like Quinn, and it wasn't favorable. They thought Easterners believed themselves their intellectual superiors, regarding their western brethren with contempt. I wondered if Quinn was even aware of the adverse effect his candid manner was having on the small-town sheriff, or if he was perfectly aware of it, and did it anyway.

"What can I do for you, Mister Quinn?" Hobson asked, in a tone that clearly conveyed his wish for Quinn to move along as soon as possible.

"If you insist." Quinn looked over at me and then back at Hobson. "I wish to have a word with you, sheriff, regarding the treatment of this man whom you have in custody. You see, I thought it best to speak with you confidentially – one lawman to another."

"Lawman?" Hobson said with raised eyebrows.

"Yes. I was once an agent for the Department of the Treasury. Now I work for the Pinkertons." Quinn paused as if to let Hobson digest that for a moment. "You have heard that name before, I expect."

Hobson nodded, suspiciously. "You have anything backing up that claim?"

"Certainly." Quinn shrugged, opening his coat and reaching inside.

Hobson suddenly backed away as if in fear. I was confused by this, until I saw that a large pistol hung from a holster slung under Quinn's left armpit. Hobson was not wearing a weapon – a good practice for any keeper of a jail house, in the event he accidentally ventured too close to the bars of the cells – and he froze momentarily until it was clear Quinn was not reaching for the newly revealed weapon, but a leather fold in an inside pocket. From it, Quinn produced an official-looking document that, if not entirely corroborating his association with the famous detective agency, at least confused Hobson enough to squelch any more questions about his identity.

After Hobson nodded, Quinn returned the credentials to the fold and buttoned up his coat again, saying nothing about the concealed weapon.

"As I was saying, sheriff. As a career man of the law, I find it my duty to provide guidance and advice whenever I see the law not being properly enforced in these remote western territories. I know it is purely innocent on your part, but there are some due processes that must be followed from the paved streets of New York City to the dusty hamlets of Arizona."

"What?" Hobson seemed confused.

"How long have you been a law officer, Sheriff Hobson?"

"Two years now?"

"And your occupation before that?" Quinn asked, almost as an accusation. "Was it in law enforcement?"

After some hesitation, Hobson shook his head.

"I didn't think so. So, I assume this is your first position as a lawman?"

"Just what is this all about?" Hobson demanded, clearly becoming irritated by the probing questions and Quinn's manner.

"I don't mean to encroach on your jurisdiction, sheriff, but when I see a man, still behind bars, nearly twelve hours after he was wrongly arrested for an act that was clearly in self-defense, then I must conclude the local law enforcement establishment does not quite understand the letter of the laws they are to uphold. This man should have been released as soon as it was established that he acted in self-defense."

"What?" Hobson retorted. "Self-defense? This murderer?"

Quinn screwed up his face. "Murderer, sheriff? I can assure you, the man he shot is very much alive. In fact, I observed him in the saloon this very evening, albeit with a bandaged shoulder."

Obviously realizing he had said too much, Hobson moved quickly to cover his tracks. "I meant attempted murderer. He very well could have killed Frank Garfield with that bullet."

"Come now, sheriff. I know very little about your prisoner, here, but I saw the whole thing, and it was clear to me that his bullet went exactly where he meant for it to go. If he had wanted to kill Garfield, he could have done it. In fact, I believe he showed great restraint. There would have been a strong case for self-defense, even if he had killed Mister Garfield. He should be released, at once."

"Well, he's not going anywhere. He's dangerous, and he's going to stay right there in that cell where he belongs."

"Being dangerous is not a crime, sheriff." Quinn said, his face turning suddenly grave. "Really, sheriff, I must insist. You will release him."

"Young fella," Hobson said, inching closer to the rack of rifles on the wall. "Around here, we don't take kindly to people telling us how to run our town."

"You know, I thought that might be your response, sheriff," Quinn smiled. "I've dealt with your kind before, sadly. You frontier lawmen are always a little reluctant to adopt the proven methods in favor of the easier, more barbaric ways. But, isn't that the very thing we're trying to bring to this untamed land, sheriff - civilization and order?"

My gunfighter instinct detected a sudden change in Hobson's demeanor. His shifty eyes told me crazy ideas were swirling in his head. He eyed the gun rack, then looked back at Quinn, clearly judging whether he could reach for the shotgun and use it before the Pinkerton man could get to his own weapon, now buttoned up in his coat. Quinn was casually looking around the room, and it was not clear to me that he had noticed the sheriff's hand slowly moving toward the gun rack. I was about to call out a warning to him, when he spoke again.

"It's only right that you should know this, sheriff, but I took the liberty of sending off a telegram this afternoon."

Hobson dropped his hand, a confused look crossing his face. "A telegram?"

"Yes. To a friend of mine in Prescott, a lawman – John Fostman. Surely, you've heard of him. He's the new U.S. marshal appointed to the territory, approved by Congress and endorsed by the 11th Arizona Territorial Legislature just last month. Have you not heard?"

"Fostman?" Hobson said, incredulously. The cigarette nearly dropped from Hobson's mouth as he stared back at him. Evidently, Martinique's tentacles did not reach as far as the U.S. Marshal.

"You have heard of him, then. In my telegram, I told him there was a small-town sheriff here in Dougson, in over his head. I told him this amateur sheriff had made a questionable arrest and was detaining a man who, by my reckoning, was entirely innocent. I suggested to the marshal that you could probably use a little guidance from someone of his experience and renown. As you probably know, Marshal Fostman is ever duty-bound and punctual. I'm sure he'll be along in a few days and clear this whole matter up." Quinn glanced at me again, then back at Hobson. "Of course, if you were to release Mister Jones, right now, I could send off another telegram telling the marshal not to bother about it. I'd send it first thing in the morning, just as soon as the telegraph office opens. With any luck, it would catch up with the marshal before he sets out."

Hobson stared back at Quinn open-mouthed, evidently grappling with which course of action would incense Martinique more. Keeping me under arrest and risking the marshal's involvement, or letting me get away, and, with me, the information they believed I had.

After a long pause spent casting doubtful glances at Quinn, Hobson finally sighed exasperatedly. He reached inside a drawer and removed a set of large keys, and then the shotgun from the rack. He had evidently decided on the latter option, and that was probably the wisest choice for him. Martinique could always have me apprehended again, once the threat of U.S. Marshal involvement had been averted.

The Pinkerton man looked smugger than ever, as Hobson grudgingly unlocked and opened the door to my cell.

CHAPTER IX   Brains and Lead

"There he goes," Quinn whispered from the darkness, flashing a white-toothed grin at me.

From an unlit corner across the street, both of us watched as Sheriff Hobson emerged from the jail house. Hobson was panicky, fumbling with his keys, his coat half on, his hat askew. After a quick scan of the dark street, in which he did not appear to see us, Hobson pocketed the keys and rushed along as fast as his short legs could carry him, making directly for the livery stable, the next building over. Shortly after disappearing inside, he emerged again, this time leading a horse. In seconds, he was in the saddle and had galloped off into the darkness.

Quinn and I had left the jail not yet five minutes ago, and now the puppet sheriff was leaving town.

"One guess where he's headed in such a hurry," Quinn said.

"Off to tell his master, I expect."

Quinn nodded. "That's my bet, too. It'll take some time. From what I have learned in my brief time here, Martinique's ranch is a good two hours' ride away. But you can bet Martinique will send every man he has." He paused, and then looked at me, as if he had forgotten something. "I'm sorry, we haven't been properly introduced. My name is Allen Quinn. I know your name, Mister Jones, only because your arrest was the talk of the saloon this afternoon. Very good to meet you."

"I owe you thanks," I replied, shaking his hand. "Though I'm not sure why you helped me. Do you make a habit of getting involved in other people's business?"

He smiled behind the mustache. "Not a habit, Mister Jones, an occupation. I'm a private investigator of sorts, a bookworm with muscle, if you will." He patted the lump in his coat under his left arm. "Brains and lead, I like to say."

"Well, one word of advice to you, Mister Quinn. If you're going to stay around these parts much longer, you better put that gun where you can get to it. Out here, no one's going to be courteous enough to wait for you to unbutton your coat."

He looked at me as though I had suggested he wear his shoes on the wrong feet. "I've found, Mister Jones, that brandishing a weapon simply courts trouble. Few men perceive an unarmed man as a threat, and even fewer would challenge one to a duel."

"And what about the ones that just want you dead?"

He looked at me with amused eyes behind his spectacles, glancing once at the sidearm on my hip. "Considering your own gun landed you in jail only this afternoon, Mister Jones, I think I might have the firmer ground in this debate."

I smiled, patting the pommel of my weapon. It felt good to be armed, like I was whole again. Without any legal means for retaining them, and after Quinn issued more threats of the looming U.S. Marshal, Sheriff Hobson had returned my gun, hat, coat, and other accoutrements. What was more, according to the sheriff, my horse and saddle were quartered in the same stable from which Hobson had just retrieved his own, and I was now free to reclaim them.

"Though, in all fairness," Quinn continued. "I don't think Hobson arrested you because you shot that man on the street."

I studied him curiously. I had assumed this oddly-dressed detective to be nothing more than a simple idealist crusader of the law, roaming the countryside to see that justice was upheld, but I was beginning to think his involvement in this matter might go further than that.

"Why, then?" I asked, wanting to see what he knew.

"I believe the sheriff arrested you because his boss desired it."

"His boss?"

Quinn nodded. "A man by the name of Pierre T. Martinique, a big man in this country. He's the same man you saw blackmailing that rancher in the saloon earlier today."

"Mister Martinique and I have met," I replied. "He paid me a visit in the jail."

"That does not surprise me in the least. Then I'm quite certain he asked you about this." Quinn drew an object from his coat, and held it up in the scant lighting.

It was the wooden cross, the etched characters across its face drawing shallow shadows.

"You were the one who took it from me?" I asked astonished. For, it had never occurred to me that this well-dressed easterner might be the culprit.

He nodded. "And it was no small feat, either, with all those elbows, boots, and spurs flying. I came near to catching a few with my face."

"Then you know its worth?" I asked. "You know why Martinique wants it so badly?"

"No," he replied sullenly. "I'm afraid I don't. I was hoping you might shed some light on that for me."

"Is that why you sprung me from jail?"

"One of the reasons, yes. You see, Jones, I was sent here by the Catholic Church to look into a matter between the San Miguel parish and our friend Mister Martinique. I was sent here quite in the blind, without full knowledge of the details of the dispute, simply because the details were not available at the time of my departure."

"The church sent you?"

"Yes, the Archdiocese of Baltimore to be precise. A month ago, the archbishop received a letter from Father Perez, the head priest of the San Miguel parish. The letter was sent by special courier, the matter being too sensitive to be conveyed in the mail or over the wires. In the letter, the priest requested help in dealing with a local land baron named Martinique. It seems Mister Martinique has been hounding him over some age-old property ownership dispute. Beyond that, the letter did not specify the property in question. I work for a firm in Baltimore that has done several odd jobs for the archdiocese, over the years, all of them discreet affairs. Thus, our services were enlisted in this matter. I was commissioned to travel out West and provide my unique services to Father Perez and the San Miguel parish. I arrived in town only yesterday."

"Then you're not with the Pinkertons."

"Not exactly." He paused, as if considering whether he should say any more. "Actually, not at all, though I have worked with them on several occasions."

I chuckled for a long moment. Quinn looked at me oddly, as if trying to decide whether it was his charade or the idea that he might be a Pinkerton that I found so amusing.

"Incidentally," he continued, slightly perturbed, "I arrived in Flagstaff by train, four days ago, and chartered a horse to ride directly here. I rode straight out to the mission, without coming into town, hoping to contact Father Perez and keep my presence here confidential. But as I approached the mission, I could see it was being watched by at least two men. Neither looked friendly. I stayed out of sight, not knowing whether they were friends of Martinique or the church. I watched the mission most of the day, but saw little to enlighten me. It appeared largely deserted. No bells ringing. No chanted prayers. The few parishioners visiting were searched by the two men, which leads me to believe they were Martinique's men, no doubt searching for this cross. Anyone going in or coming out of the church grounds was searched without exception. Baskets, blankets, everything, even the clothes off their backs. One poor woman, who clearly did not speak

English, tried to resist and was struck down by the scoundrels. They laughed as they stripped her naked, and searched the folds of her garments, tearing them in the process. By the time her clothes were returned to her, her dress was in tatters. She left sobbing, and muttering curses in Spanish under her breath. I would have intervened at that moment had I not a duty to fulfill to the archbishop. The only people I saw who I did not see coming or going, so I assume they dwell there, were an old man and a young woman. I saw them come out of one of the outbuildings to draw water from the well in the plaza. They then disappeared again, just as quickly. I can only assume the priests are in hiding, or they've gone off on some excursion dictated by their profession. I considered waiting for their return, but I – "

"They will not be returning," I said solemnly. "They're dead."

"Dead!" he exasperated.

"I came across their bodies up on the plateau, three days ago. They had been ambushed. Six killed in all. Some had been tortured before they died."

"What the hell were they doing there?"

"They looked to be heading east, packed for a very long trip."

"The fools!" Quinn exclaimed, clearly frustrated. "Why didn't they stay put? The archbishop sent them a telegram instructing them to stay put!"

I shrugged. "Maybe Martinique owns the telegraph office, as well. Maybe that message never reached them. In any event, it was definitely Martinique's men that attacked them. They ransacked the baggage and the carts, I suppose looking for that." I pointed at the cross in his hand. "It was just by chance I came along when I did. I think I must have scared the bastards off before they had finished their handiwork. I found that cross near the body of one of the priests."

"Damn!" Quinn stared off into the darkness as if pondering what to do next.

"I'm unclear about something," I ventured, after a long moment of silence. "If you're so much in the dark about this whole affair, why did you take the cross from me during the dust-up? How did you know Martinique wanted it?"

Quinn was only half listening. The news of the priests' deaths had struck him quite speechless. He looked drained of all animation, as a man who had just lost his life's fortune in a single spin of the roulette wheel. It was some time before he answered.

"One can learn a lot just sitting in a public establishment, playing a tune," he said wearily. "After leaving San Miguel, I rode into town, found that saloon, and sat and played, acting as though I was a simple weary traveler. Over the years, I've trained my ears to filter out the conversations I don't want to hear, that I might eavesdrop on others. After a few hours of playing, I had heard and seen enough interesting things regarding Mister Martinique to conclude unequivocally that he has nearly every man in town under his thumb in one way or another. Then I saw you walk in, an obvious stranger. I heard you mention San Miguel, saw you show the cross, and saw the bartender's reaction. I had been watching that fool all morning, and nothing made him lose so much color as when you presented this little item. When he scurried away, obviously to inform his boss, I deduced the cross was something of importance, something Martinique desperately wanted, though I hadn't a clue as to why. I still don't." He paused, looking at me hopefully. "I suppose you've already told me all you know about it. Is there anything else?"

"Sorry, no."

He nodded and stared at the object, turning it over in his hands, as if it might speak to him. "Why the devil would a man murder six men – six men of the cloth – over something so trivial as this?" But at that moment, as he gazed at the cross, his eyes suddenly grew wider. "Hello...what's this?"

His finger had found a small groove in the cross piece, its shadow just visible when held at a certain angle in the light of the lantern. It was as fine as a strand of hair. As I watched, Quinn took out a small pocket knife and used it to pry it into the groove. This opened a small chamber in the cross, no larger than a woman's little finger.

"It's a secret panel, only..." he paused.

"What?"

"It's empty," he said, suddenly disheartened again. "I assume whatever Martinique wants was in here, at some point, but it's gone now."

"Well, I wish you luck," I stammered, considering this as good an opportunity as any to take my leave. "You've got that cross, and you know about the murders. That's all you need from me, I expect. I suppose I'll be moseying along now. I'm much obliged to you for springing me from jail. Maybe I can return the favor someday."

He looked at me in disbelief. "You don't mean you're going to just up and leave at a time like this!"

"That's exactly what I mean. I've worn out my welcome here. This isn't my fight. I've got a mule train of goods to sell in the Verde Valley. I've lost enough time as it is. If you need any statement from me about the priests' death, I'll be glad to do it. But, there's no reason for me to stick around."

"Look, Jones, I don't need your statement, at least not yet. The other reason I broke you out of jail was I need someone I can trust. More importantly, I need someone who's good with the gun. I've a feeling I'm going to go up against Martinique and his hired hands before all this is over. I can't handle them alone."

"What about your friend, the U.S. Marshal? Why don't you send him a telegraph in the morning telling him to bring some deputies with him? Then you can sit tight until your friend arrives."

Quinn's eyes went to the ground, almost as if in shame. "I never sent the telegram."

"What?" I replied in astonishment.

"I lied. Do I have to say it? The marshal isn't coming. I don't even know him."

"Then how in the hell did you –"

"I read an editorial in a paper I picked up in Flagstaff. The marshal's name was mentioned, and I made a mental note of it. It's an old trick of the trade."

I looked at him in disbelief. If that ruse had not worked, I'd still be in jail, and quite possibly lynched before the week was out.

"I don't think the archbishop ever conceived this affair would take such a serious turn," Quinn said soberly. "Otherwise he'd have sent a whole company of detectives." He grabbed my arm and fervently looked me in the eyes. "I need your help, Jones. The men I'm going up against are ruthless. I'm good, but not as good as you. That professional gunfighter of Martinique's is way beyond my league."

He was right about that, I thought. The musically-inclined detective could never go up against the likes of Julio, unless he wished to return to the archbishop in Baltimore as a corpse sealed inside a pine box.

"I give you my word, Jones," he continued. "You'll be compensated, more than adequately – more than you can make selling your wares in the Verde Valley. The archbishop is a generous man. What do you say?"

CHAPTER X   San Miguel

We rode through the darkness, under a brilliant field of stars, greeted from all directions by the howl of distant wolves and the hoot of the owl. The thin pine woods on either side of the trail hissed with each waft of the night wind, its breath carrying a chill to make us button our coats up tighter.

Having retrieved my horse and saddle, we had first ridden to the Johnstone Livery Stable on the outskirts of Dougson where I had boarded my mules. Quinn had protested the whole way, arguing that Martinique might very well send a band of gunmen to San Miguel as soon as word reached him of my release, and, if that were the case, we would have little time to get to the mission before they did. But there was something I had to retrieve from my packs, aside from my rifle and a few boxes of ammunition – something I kept hidden from Quinn.

Not too surprising, I found my mules and packs undisturbed, and took some comfort from the fact that Martinique's men had not ransacked every stable in town - probably because there were only a few places I could have hidden the cross. I had been seen with it in the bar, and was arrested shortly thereafter. There was no way the cross could have made its way back to my trappings, and thus they had been of no interest to Martinique and his men.

It did not take long to retrieve the few items I came for, but I did so under the continual tap of Quinn's boot and the frequent examination of his pocket watch, as if such might make me move faster. Still, we made good time, pushing our horses hard, and it was only an hour later when the dark silhouette of San Miguel's bell tower blotted out the stars ahead of us.

We stopped to look and listen from a low hill nearby. As my eyes adjusted under the light of the moon, I could make out the general layout of the mission. A two-story-tall church with a bell tower acted as the anchor point in a large square of interconnected buildings, all surrounded by a waist-high wall to mark the perimeter of the church grounds. It was like many others I had seen in the southwest, constructed in the Spanish style, with adobe walls, and I imagine how intimidating it must have appeared to the Indians living here at the time of the Spanish conquest, two centuries ago. It appeared to be in a fair condition, considering its age. There were a few lights visible from three or four curtained windows among the outbuildings, but we saw no movement.

"There are people still there," Quinn whispered. "That's encouraging."

"The old man and the woman you saw yesterday?"

"Maybe." He frowned, and then added hopefully, "Or maybe some of the priests have returned. Maybe some survived the massacre."

I did not share in his optimism, but did not voice my opinion. There were other items more pressing.

"You said when you were here yesterday, there were men watching the place?"

He nodded. "Two men, that I saw, camped just outside the gate. We could circle around the mission, and go over the wall on the opposite side."

"If we do that, and they see or hear us, we won't know about it until they've snuck up on us and shot us in the back. Right now, we have surprise on our side. Let's not squander it."

We secured our horses some distance away and crept up on Martinique's hired guns. True to Quinn's word, the two men had set up camp just outside the gate marking the entrance to the mission grounds. It was clear the mission had not seen much traffic this evening, nor was any expected, because one of the ruffians lounged by a small campfire sipping coffee from a tin cup, while the other snored inside a bedroll a few paces away.

This whole business had me angry – angry enough to gun down the bastards in cold blood, but that would be unwise. There could be more out there, perhaps watching from the darkness, while these two rested.

A series of hand gestures from Quinn told me he wished to jump them from opposite sides. As he skirted around the perimeter, just outside the glow of the fire, I drew my Bowie knife from its sheath and waited for his signal.

A few moments later, a rock landed in the brush - Quinn's signal to attack. The alert man jumped to his feet, picking up his rifle in the process, and crept over to where the rock had landed.

"Get up, Mitch!" he whispered desperately to his partner. "I heard something."

As the man stared out into the darkness, I saw a shadow bolt across the clearing. The wool suit was easily recognizable in the yellow light of the campfire, and I briefly thought how absurd such clothing looked ambling through this underbrush. Though Quinn wore polished riding boots more suited for a polo match than a scuffle, he was nimble and reached the distracted man in two heartbeats, placing one well-delivered punch to the back of the man's neck. The man dropped flat on the ground and, much to my surprise, did not get back up, or even move. Quinn's single blow had knocked him out cold.

But my brief amazement was cut short by the other man, who startled awake, saw the fate of his comrade, and began scrambling from his bedroll to reach his rifle leaning against the wall nearby. I was on him before he got there, firmly planting my knee in his back and pressing him to the ground. My blood was up, the temporary insanity of the fight overtaking me, along with all the pent-up frustration of the day's events. Before I knew it, I had the struggling man by the hair, and had pulled his head back to expose his neck, while my other hand brought my knife to the stretched and bare skin.

"Jones!" Quinn shouted.

I paused, stopping the blade an instant before it would have sliced open the man's throat. I wanted to kill this man, to take out on him the anger I harbored for his boss and every other minion responsible for those innocent priests' murders and the harassment of the mission's parishioners, but Quinn was there in the next moment seizing my hand.

"We did not come here for that," he said in a scolding tone. "Don't lower yourself to their level."

I looked up at Quinn as the man quivering beneath me sobbed with fear, not knowing whether he would be spared or killed in the next breath. The eastern detective stared down at me with a pleading, genuine look of concern, and, for a moment, I remembered what the rule of law and civilized justice meant. It had been so long since I had lived under the umbrella of its protection, and his strict adherence to it was oddly refreshing. I wondered if Quinn realized I had lowered myself to their level many times in my life – the base level of western justice, in all its ugly and cruel forms. Still, Quinn's entreating stayed my hand.

After a long sigh, I struck the pommel of my knife across the back of the man's head, knocking him senseless. This was met with an approving nod from Quinn, though I was less than ecstatic about it.

"That was the right decision, Jones," he said as one might congratulate a drunk for passing up a saloon.

"Things are done differently in the West, Quinn," I replied. "Mark my words. We'll come to regret leaving these two alive. Should our paths cross again, they won't show us the same courtesy."

He smiled. "All the same, you did the right thing."

Using the pair's own ropes, we tied them up like calves ready for the branding iron. While my opponent was only

135

dazed, Quinn's was still unconscious, limp as a ragdoll, as if he had been struck by a hammer.

"Just where in the hell did you learn to do that?" I asked curiously.

Quinn grinned and held up his right hand that I might see it more clearly in the firelight. Like a set of rings across his fingers, he wore a set of metal knuckles. Whether made of brass or iron, I could not tell, but they looked much fancier and smoother than the kind I had often seen crudely molded out of bullet lead by soldiers during the war.

This detective from the east may have been a bit of an idealist – too much of an idealist, in my opinion – but he certainly was a well-armed one.

Leaving the two bound men there in the dark, with their campfire dwindling, we entered the mission grounds through the gate and approached the church warily. We had to inch our way through a graveyard full of headstones and crosses, some crumbling, some looking as old as the mission itself, some newer and dressed with dried and withered flowers. The bell tower loomed high and dark above us. Beneath it, the church's entrance was marked by a set of large wooden doors with brick-paved steps leading up to them.

If there was any proper way to enter a church in the dead of night, the main entrance seemed the most logical place.

I had drawn my gun, a lifetime of experiences telling me we were not entirely out of danger, but Quinn gestured for me to holster it, and I reluctantly complied.

The giant double-doors were each affixed with an iron ring for pulling them open or shut, and an iron knocker in the exact center. Quinn gingerly walked up the steps and rapped on the door with the lever provided. The sound seemed to reverberate in the chambers beyond.

We waited, but there was no answer.

He rapped again, this time louder, but again, no answer, no sound of footfalls within, nothing to indicate it was not deserted.

"I suppose I should try to open it," Quinn commented.

"Suit yourself," I replied, then added chidingly. "Just remember to keep that gun buttoned up inside your coat. We wouldn't want anyone to think we're looking for trouble."

Quinn shot me an annoyed glance before pushing lightly on one door. Surprisingly, it swung inward, revealing a vast dark interior within. This was to be expected, of course, when entering an empty church late at night, but what came next was entirely unforeseen. As we peered through the open door, we were suddenly confronted with the muzzle of a double-barreled shotgun emerging from the blackness and pointed directly at Quinn's mid-section.

"What do you want?" a voice demanded from the darkness beyond. It was a woman's voice, thick with a Spanish accent.

Quinn looked at the two barrels with controlled anxiety, slightly raising his hands to show he was unarmed, then removed his hat.

"Pardon me, miss," he said. "We did not mean to disturb you at such an hour, but we need to speak with the presiding priest, if we could. I'm afraid it's terribly important, otherwise –"

"Go away!" she interrupted, extending the gun in a threatening manner. "I told you before, we want nothing to do with that *villano* Martinique! Now go!"

"We're not the associates of Mister Martinique," he said, raising his hands again. "In fact, we took care of them for you. You'll find them both tied up down there."

After a long pause, in which the double-barrels remained pointed at Quinn, the woman spoke again. "You don't sound like you come from here."

"I don't ma'am. Allen Quinn's my name. The Archdiocese of Baltimore sent me."

"The archbishop?" she said, her tone briefly containing surprise, but then the muzzle shifted to point at me, and she spoke again as sternly as before. "Who's that?"

"That's Mister Jones, ma'am. He's with me."

I took off my hat and smiled politely, not sure if my manner would be taken for compliance or a threat in this darkness.

After another pause, the door opened a bit further.

"Remove your guns, and toss them to me."

We had no choice but to comply, if we wished to learn anything more from this place. After throwing our guns into the dark void, we stepped back while she retrieved them, and then we were prompted to enter.

Once inside, though we could see the church better, we knew nothing more about our guard. She wore a hooded cloak, from which the shotgun protruded, and it never ceased to point at our backs as we were directed through one turn and then another, the only light that of a candle which she had directed Quinn to hold.

We left the church through another door, crossed a dirt courtyard devoid of anything but a single, unhitched cart, a few casks, and a well with a bucket on a winch in the center. She then directed us through another door and into one of the outbuildings, the aroma of which told me it

139

served the purpose of a kitchen. There, we were met by more light, for the room was lit up by several lanterns, and a fire burning in a wood stove.

From a table in the center of the room, an old man with shaggy gray hair and a bushy, gray mustache rose to his feet, a lever-action rifle in his hands. He examined us warily as we stood there facing him, and nothing was said between us until the woman had entered and closed the door behind her.

"These two were at the door, father," she said, pushing the hood back from her face. "Mister Quinn and Mister Jones."

At my first sight of the woman's face, I forgot completely about the old man and the rifle in his hand. I had to look twice, so struck was I by her beauty. She looked to be about twenty years old, and though her brows were currently set in austerity, she had lush, dark hair, captivating brown eyes, and perfect tanned skin.

She had called the old man father, and I could immediately see that it was in the paternal rather than the religious sense, for some of her features resembled his – though they were much more pleasing on her.

"Who are they?" he asked cautiously. "Why have you brought them here?"

"They say the archbishop sent them."

"Is that true?" he asked hopefully.

"Yes," answered Quinn. "I have come in response to Father Perez's letter. I have it here, if I may."

After a permissive nod from the woman, Quinn removed the letter from the inside of his coat and presented it to the old man, who spent a long moment verifying its authenticity, and then finally waved a hand at the woman to lower her weapon. Placing his own rifle on the table, the old man smiled warmly and gestured for us to sit down.

"Esmeralda," he said to the woman. "Please fetch some wine for our guests, and some bread."

The young woman nodded, and then left through a side door, but not after casting a long searching glance in my direction. I was not sure whether the look was distrustful or simply curious in nature.

"I am Domingo Garcia" he said. "And that is my daughter, Esmeralda. I serve as the groundskeeper here, while my daughter runs the kitchen. We have attended the needs of the priests of San Miguel for many years, since Esmeralda was but a girl. I must ask your forgiveness for our cautious behavior. There are dangerous men watching this place at all hours. It amazes me that you got past them."

"Oh, we met them." I said with a knowing glance at Quinn.

After Esmeralda returned with the wine and bread, Quinn proceeded to explain his purpose here, and all that he had learned since arriving in Dougson. He allowed me to recount my experience up on the plateau, and the terrible fate of the priests. It was immensely difficult for me to tell them all the details, not because I was having trouble remembering, but because it seemed to affect Esmeralda so. Both she and her father let down their guard in a deflated moment of grief and despair, each crossing themselves, and hugging each other in anguish, tears dripping down their cheeks for the priests they had once known and loved.

But, after a few minutes of silence, while Garcia still appeared stricken with only grief, I saw something else form in his daughter's eyes, an emotion I myself was quite familiar with and thus could easily recognize in others. With her eyes still wet with tears, her face began to transform from that of one in mourning to that of one consumed with anger, and a look of determination that she would make sure the men responsible for the priests' deaths paid for what they had done.

"Poor old Father Perez," Garcia finally said, sitting back heavily in his chair. "I told him not to go. I begged him not to go. The other priests begged him as well. We knew the trail would be treacherous, but even I misjudged how desperate Martinique has become. Now, all that the father struggled to protect all these years is lost." He paused as if it were difficult to continue. "Father Perez baptized Esmeralda. Oh, my child. What kind of animals can do such a thing?"

Again, the old man broke down into a fit of tears, covering his face with his hands. Quinn had not yet revealed that he was in possession of the cross. He then opened his coat, took out the cross, presented it before Garcia's streaming eyes, and then placed it on the table.

"We believe they were after this" Quinn said. "Do you know what it is? Do you know its significance?"

The room was suddenly silent. For both Garcia and his daughter had instantly ceased crying, and now gazed in open-mouthed astonishment at the cross on the table as if it were the Holy Grail.

CHAPTER XI   Padre De Oro

The sight of the wooden cross on the table had left Garcia and his daughter dumbstruck. They looked at each other with questioning eyes as if each was uncertain whether they should share any more information.

Quinn, seeing them suddenly distrustful again, spoke in a reassuring tone. "As I said before, I was sent here by the archbishop to help Father Perez and his associates. I regret having arrived too late for that, but we may yet be able to prevent Martinique from acquiring what he wanted from the good priest, presumably this cross, or what it represents. We owe it to Father Perez and the other priests to see it does not end up in Martinique's hands." Quinn paused, letting his words sink in. "But I can only succeed in that endeavor if I know more. Can you tell us the significance of this object? Do you know why Martinique desires it?"

The old man seemed to consider for a long time as he stared first at Quinn, then at me, and finally at his daughter who seemed even more reluctant and shook her head as if to stop him from saying anything more.

"Do not tell them father," she said looking at us skeptically. "They have a letter from the archbishop, but we don't know anything about these two. They could have been sent by Martinique. It could all be an elaborate trick." She pointed at me. "This one smiles as though he knows something. I can tell he's hiding something. For all we know he was the one that murdered Father Perez. I have told you before father, I can always smell death on a man."

I did not know if this alluring, young woman had some strange power of observation, or if she was just guessing, but she was right. I was hiding something. Perhaps my previous life as a hired gun, and thus a killer, was evident in my manner. As I had seen and recognized it in Julio, she had seen it in me. When I made no response to her allegation, other than to remove the smile from my face, she seemed somewhat confused. She stared into my eyes for a long moment, and the longer she stared, the more her own expression softened, as if she was more convinced with each passing moment that I had no part in the priests' murder, and she regretted ever accusing me of such. Though she said nothing, she seemed apologetic, clearly aware that she had gone too far.

Regardless, her father was not swayed by her former opinion.

"I have lived many years, Esmeralda." Garcia said. "I have learned to judge a man very quickly, and, usually, my judgment is correct. I do not know these two, but I know they are telling us the truth. The shadow of evil does not follow them as it does Martinique's men. We must trust someone to help us. Now that these two gentlemen have brought us that," he pointed at the cross on the table, "I say, we trust them."

Sitting up in his chair, the old man reached out to touch the wooden object. He turned it over in his hands several times, not as though he were inspecting it, but as if stirred fond memories of the late priest. Then, quite suddenly, he flipped the cross over, took out a small knife, and used it to pry open the hidden panel on the backside.

Quinn exchanged glances with me, before exclaiming, "A secret compartment! Why didn't I see that before?"

The detective was being a bit too dramatic for my liking, but he clearly did not want to let on that we had already discovered that feature.

"It was hidden very skillfully, by a master woodworker," Garcia said, smiling. "I made this cross myself, many years ago, for Father Perez. I added this compartment that he might write down a prayer or devotion and carry it close to his heart. I did not conceive back then that it would someday be used for a much different purpose."

But after the panel was removed and Domingo held the cross closer to the candle on the table, he let out a long, exasperated sigh, as if he had just lost any hope that remained within him.

"It is not here! It is not here!" he exclaimed. "Martinique must have it! It is terrible, Esmeralda! Terrible! Father Perez, and all the others, they died for nothing!"

Quinn and I exchanged questioning looks, before Quinn finally said. "What did you expect to find, Mister Garcia?"

Again, the old man looked hesitant, but eventually closed his eyes and nodded his head. He looked at his daughter. "Esmeralda, fetch the keys."

"Father, no!" she protested. "We cannot trust these men."

"Fetch the keys, daughter!' he said more firmly. "It is time they know. Perhaps they can help recover what we have lost."

After a long sigh, Esmeralda disappeared for a few moments out the side door. When she returned, she held a small iron key that appeared as old as the mission itself. She cradled it between both hands, as if it were something sacred. With some pause, she handed it to her father. The

147

old man rose and crossed to the other side of the room, gesturing for us to help him move a bookshelf out of the way to reveal an indentation in the side of the adobe wall. The old man felt around until he found what he was looking for – three finger holes which he used to pry and pivot the door open. It wasn't really a door at all. It was just a false wall. But behind it was a heavy wooden door with a keyhole lock. After several attempts with the key, the clicking and crunching lock finally moved, and the door opened into a black void beyond.

Garcia motioned for us to bring the lanterns and led us into the dark space. We were immediately met by a steep staircase leading down into a narrow tunnel. As we descended, the air turned frigid. The tunnel was tight enough that I had to stoop to get through it but once we had gone down what must have been two flights of stairs we were deposited into a room.

As the light of the lantern revealed our surroundings, I saw that the room was quite small, like a storeroom for cold goods. But this room contained no stores that I could see, only a collection of neatly stacked crates against one wall, and a single table in the center of the room on which stood a large half-depleted candle with streams of solidified wax running down its sides and connecting to solid white pools on the table beneath.

On the opposite side of the room, another passage led off into unknown blackness, from which cool air wafted steadily.

"This is a private place," Garcia said, "dating back to the construction of the mission, in the year of Our Lord 1699. Its existence has been a carefully guarded secret, passed down from priest to priest over the generations. Only a few others knew about it."

"What's so important about it?" I asked, my tone unimpressed, for I could not imagine the significance of the room. It looked like nothing more than a private study for the priests to pray undisturbed, or pen their next sermon.

Garcia then held the lantern closer to the stacked objects which I had taken for wooden crates, and now I saw what they truly were. Both Quinn and I gasped. They were not crates, but chests, overlaid in tooled leather and elaborately adorned with iron ornamentation. I had not seen their like before, but something told me they were from the early days of the mission.

Quinn seemed more stunned than I was. He immediately walked over to examine them, running his hands along the groves in the leather.

"Incredible!" he exclaimed. "I've only seen such things in the homes of a few people – very wealthy people." He paused, then added. "As antiques. These chests are hundreds of years old. These designs are from the Spanish colonial era."

"That is correct, Mister Quinn," Garcia replied.

Quinn reached for the iron clasp of the chest nearest him, cast one uncertain look back at the old man, then slid open the creaking metal hinge and raised the lid. After a long study of the dark cavity within, he turned back to look at Garcia. "Are they all empty, as this one is?"

Garcia nodded.

The detective shook his head. "While they are exquisite, and most remarkable, I highly doubt a man like Martinique would commit murder just to get his hands on a few antiques, which could, at most, fetch him a few hundred dollars."

"It is not the chests Martinique is after," Garcia replied. "It is what they once carried. Two hundred years ago, when the conquistadores came to these lands, a certain officer, a lieutenant to the Spanish colonial governor Juan de Ornate, discovered a rich gold deposit in the desert mountains southeast of here. He kept its location a secret, but enlisted the aid of a corrupt Franciscan priest named Juan del

Castillo, and the two devised a plan to extract the gold for themselves. Under the premise of bringing Christianity to the native people, they established the San Miguel mission, a façade for their own private mining operation, and soon shipments of gold were heading south in large quantities. At that time, this mission was so remote – nearly four hundred miles from the colonial capital in Santa Fe – that it was not difficult to keep such an operation a secret. They brought in Pueblo peoples as slave labor and discouraged visitors through exaggerated stories of savage Apache raids.

"But Father Castillo was more of a scoundrel than the officer, looking to secure a fortune for himself above all. He oversaw the construction of the mission while the officer saw to the mine. While the officer was away for several months, Castillo had this tunnel excavated and this chamber created to serve as his personal storeroom. Once the construction was complete, he dismissed the workers to far off lands and told no one of its existence, save for a few in his inner circle. There were twenty-four caravans that took the gold south, one every month for two years. From each caravan, Castillo arranged to have one crate of gold spirited away without the knowledge of his business partner, and, over time, amassed twenty-four crates of gold in this room – a great fortune, nonetheless. But, so much gold cannot remain a secret for long, and eventually everyone from the parishioners to the slaves were whispering of the priest who was richer than a sultan. They began to refer to him as Padre de Oro – the Father of Gold.

"The Spanish officer may have suspected his partner's deception, but he never got the chance to act on it. Shortly after the last caravan, Father Castillo suffered a stroke that confined him to bed. At the same time, the officer was recalled to Spain, and, fearful his illicit operation would be found out, had the mine destroyed and all the mine workers killed. To this day, no one knows its location.

"Juan del Castillo lingered for ten days, during which he never rose from his bed. But it is believed his nearness to death inspired a change of heart in him in those last days. For the first time, he had a genuine prayer on his lips for the souls of his parishioners and the native people of this land. The night before he died, he claimed to have had a vision, in which he saw twenty-four angels who instructed him that this gold should not be sent to far off Europe, but should be preserved to enrich the lives of the natives who scarcely understood its worth. He commended this charge to the priest who succeeded him as the last rites were read. The gold was to remain here, a secret within these catacombs, waiting for generations to serve the people to whom it truly belonged." He sighed heavily. "That was two hundred years ago. Obviously, things changed in Spain, as they did here. The Spanish largely abandoned this region, leaving behind the missions, many of which were also abandoned after countless Indian raids. But, San Miguel survived. Over time, rumors of the gold passed from memory into legend, and the legacy handed down to subsequent priests of this parish, to fervently protect the hidden gold and keep its existence secret. The line of priests was never broken." He paused, appearing choked with grief, before adding, "Our own Father Perez was the last to be charged with this great duty."

"But the chests are empty," Quinn said.

Garcia nodded. "Recently, the rumor of the gold's existence resurfaced outside these walls. It has long been suspected this was the fault of the groundskeeper before me, a drunk who was dismissed over his devotion to the bottle. Within a week, he had drunk himself to death, spending every last penny he had saved in the priest's service. He died, but not before he managed to blather the secrets of the mission in every saloon within a hundred miles. It became clear to Father Perez that the gold must be removed from the mission, for he knew it was only a matter

153

of time before the rumors reached the ears of someone who might act on them. All the priests of the mission were sworn to secrecy, as was I, and we slowly ferried the gold to another location, far from here. We traveled at night, and agreed to be blindfolded during the day that we might never know the true location. Only Father Perez knew it, and he guided us."

"And you have no idea where it is?" I asked, perhaps a bit too eagerly.

Garcia shook his head. "It took us a week to get there, loaded down with the gold. It is hidden inside a cave amongst some ancient ruins. I can say no more, for I know no more. That was years ago. For many years after that, we lived in peace, and began to hope the secret was still safe. Then, a few months ago, Martinique began taking a sudden interest in the mission, claiming the property belonged to his spread, and that he had the documentation to prove it. He demanded that the church and everything in it were his, and that nothing could be removed without his express permission. It became clear to Father Perez that Martinique must know about the gold, for this land would be of little use for raising cattle. Martinique even made an offer to build a new mission for us, many miles from here, but Father Perez refused. Many of the other priests thought that foolish since the gold had already been removed, but Father Perez stood his ground on principle.

"In response to the rejection, Martinique made life within these walls miserable, for us and our parishioners. He stationed men to watch us day and night, and soon after that, most of the parishioners stopped coming. The sheriff in Dougson did nothing to stop it. Everyone knows he is paid by Martinique. The other priests suggested calling on the U.S. Marshall, but Father Perez did not want to bring anyone else into this matter. He believed once it was widely known what the mission had contained, every gold-chaser in the country would come looking for it. Father Perez used to always say *gold is the bait by which the evil one lures men to their dooms*. He was adamant that this should remain within the church. So, he sent a letter to the archbishop in Baltimore, asking for assistance." Garcia looked bleakly at Quinn. "I suppose you are the answer to that letter, Mister Quinn. But, now, Father Perez is dead, and Martinique has the map."

"Map?" Quinn prompted. "What map?"

"The map to the gold, the only written record of its hiding place. Father Perez inscribed it onto a linen cloth, and kept it rolled up beneath this panel." He gestured to the disassembled cross. "It never left his person. His murderers must have found the hidden panel, and that means they have the map."

Quinn looked stunned for a moment at this new revelation, but, after a few moments of consideration, picked up the cross and studied the panel.

"Why would they have put the panel back in place?" Quinn asked to no one in particular, then looked at me. "Jones, when you found this thing, was it in two pieces?"

I shook my head.

Quinn looked back at the old man. "There, you see? Martinique's men would not have bothered to put the cross back together after removing the map. Besides, Martinique is after the cross. He questioned Jones, here, about it only a few hours ago. Clearly, Martinique doesn't have the map."

At this revelation, the old man's face brightened up, and he looked at his daughter with hope. "Could it be, Esmeralda? The old father has tricked these evil men again? Could he have hidden the map somewhere else?"

"He must have, father." She glanced at me uncomfortably, as if still not entirely willing to trust us.

"If this is true," Garcia said, "then we must find it first. We must go to the scene of that terrible act, and look for the map, and we must leave at once."

"Have you lost all your senses?" Quinn retorted. "This matter has escalated beyond a simple property dispute. We're talking about murder now, Mister Garcia. Martinique is willing to kill for this gold of yours. He'll have the trails watched, just as he's had this place watched. They'll stay out of sight until you've found the map, and then kill you, and take it from you." He glanced once at Esmeralda, but the young woman appeared just as resolved as her father. "You and your daughter are key witnesses to what's been going on here. It is too much of a risk. As the acting agent of the archbishop, I demand that you and your daughter accompany me to Flagstaff, where we will get on the first eastbound train. We will put all of this before the archbishop, and let him decide how to proceed."

"No!" Garcia shook his head. "The map must not fall into the hands of Martinique! If he finds the map, he will find the gold, and then our friends will have died for nothing! We must find it before he does."

"Please, listen to reason, sir."

"You cannot stop us, Mister Quinn. My daughter and I were devoted to Father Perez and the others. We will see their task completed. We will set out at first light. If you choose to come with us, you may. If not, we will find the map ourselves."

"There must be another way," Quinn said, clearly frustrated.

"There is no other way," Garcia retorted.

"I'm telling you, Mister Garcia, you are being completely –"

At that moment, both men stopped talking. They gazed with astonishment at the table, where I had just placed something I had removed from my coat pocket. Esmeralda, too, joined them in staring open-mouthed at the unfolded piece of linen before them.

"Ladies and gentlemen," I said with a casual smile, though I still wasn't sure I had made the right decision. "May I present to you, the map."

CHAPTER XII   Thou Shalt Not Kill

"Ciudadela," Quinn said, studying the map under the light of the lantern. "What's that?"

"It is a set of ruins, up on the plateau," Garcia answered with delight, as he had suspected the gold was located there all along. "It is a three-day ride from here."

"I presume this map then shows where the gold is hidden amongst the ruins?" Quinn asked, pointing to the line scrawled onto the linen that snaked between what appeared to be square-shaped buildings and followed a creek to a large "X" marked at its head.

Garcia put his glasses on to examine it. "Yes, yes. That is as I remember it. The creek was nearly dry when I was there. It is fed by a natural spring. The cave is at the source of the spring. That is where the gold is hidden. I have no doubt."

Quinn sighed and stared at the map, as if this new information changed all his plans. He cast a look across the table at me, clearly somewhat frustrated that I had not shared it with him before.

"It is late, gentlemen," Garcia said. "And I believe we will be up for several more hours discussing this. Esmeralda, some coffee, please."

After a glance in my direction, which conveyed more disenchantment than Quinn's had, Esmeralda rose obediently, grabbed two buckets from the sideboard, and exited through the door. Not wishing to hear any of Quinn's frustrations put to words, I slipped out a few seconds after her.

I followed with the intent to help her, as well as look out for her, but when I reached the moonlit courtyard, I saw that she had stopped half-way to the well, the buckets still held in both hands. She stood there, her shoulders trembling, and I got the sense that she had waited until she was alone, out of the sight of her father, to break down and cry over the loss of the priests. She sobbed openly and audibly, quite unaware that I was there.

I did not wish to startle nor embarrass her, so I waited a few minutes longer, then made sure my boots could be heard on the planks of the boardwalk surrounding the plaza. Before I emerged from the shadows, I saw her set one bucket on the ground then wipe the tears from her eyes with one hand. When she finally turned to face me, she had restored her hitherto defiant expression to some extent.

"What are you doing here?" she said in an annoyed tone.

"I thought you might need some help," I smiled. "You're loaded down a mite."

"I can manage it myself," she replied dismissively.

"It isn't safe."

"Then you and your companion should go!" she said hotly. "My father and I do not need your help. We do not want your kind around."

"My kind?"

She looked up into my eyes defiantly. There was no fear in her, and it was clear to me she had been forced to hold her own many times before, likely under the bullying and chastisement of Martinique's men, whenever she and her father were forced to go into town for supplies.

"Your kind brings death everywhere you go."

"But, today, my kind brought you hope," I said light-heartedly. "I brought you the priest's map."

Her eyes narrowed. "Tell me, Mister Jones. Why did Mister Quinn not know the map was in your possession? Why had you not told him about it?"

I said nothing, but her expression told me she had already surmised the answer. Why had I kept the map a secret? It was simple, really. I was hoping to secure the gold for myself. I had come upon that secret chamber while fiddling with the cross the night after I had retrieved it from beside the dead priest's body. I had found the map, saw it was something of importance, pocketed it, and then carefully replaced the panel. Before entering Dougson, I had hidden the map amongst my packs in the livery stable, in the event I got so drunk – as I was wont to do, on occasion – that I lost it. When I presented the cross to the bartender in the saloon yesterday, it was with hopes of learning more about what the map led to. When I saw his reaction, I knew I had a rare find. Yes, after being sprung from jail, I had agreed to help Quinn for purely selfish reasons. I saw a way for me to learn more about the map's purpose, and I shamelessly took it. I had intended to leave the Baltimore detective behind once I had learned what treasure lay at the spot marked on the map. I said before, I was not a church-goer. I was a desperate man, scratching and fighting to get ahead, to have enough riches that I could set myself up right with a ranch of my own, somewhere where I would never cross paths with my old opponents – like Frank Garfield and Julio. I had not cared about Quinn, the mission, Martinique, or any promises made by some centuries dead priest to angels in a vision. I had come to San Miguel intending to fool them all – to make off with the gold myself.

So, if all that was true, then why had I finally revealed the map to these people? That was simple, too. I was looking into the glistening, beautiful, brown and perfect eyes of the reason, right now.

"Yes, I know well your kind, Mister Jones," Esmeralda said, though without as much venom as before. Perhaps she had detected the affection in my own eyes as they stared back into hers.

I smiled, and then took a rolled cigarette from my pocket, struck a match along the post to light it, and placed it between my lips. Then I stooped to take the buckets from her hands, our skin touching for the briefest instant.

"I've come here to help you," I said warmly. "You have nothing to fear from me."

She paused, and seemed to be momentarily affected by the contact of our hands. I saw her involuntarily let her guard down, though she tried ardently to keep up the rigid exterior. "I assure you, Mister Jones, I am not afraid of –"

She was cut short by the report of a gun and the ricochet of a bullet off the stone works above the well. Grabbing her arm, I jerked her down behind the well with me just as another fusillade of bullets struck all around us. We stared at each other, still breathing hard, still fazed by the suddenness of the attack. I did not know for certain who was out there, trying to kill us, but I would have bet all my packs and mules on one guess. For her part, Esmeralda was brave. She made no outburst, but simply ducked her head whenever I told her to keep down.

Off to the right, dark shapes moved near the church. Several of our assailants were trying to get around behind us. I would have liked to send some lead in their direction. I would have liked to stop them, but I could not. I was unarmed. My weapon was still on the table in the kitchen house.

At that moment, I cursed Quinn for letting Esmeralda disarm us. There was only one choice for us now.

"Can you run?" I asked her.

She nodded.

"When I give the word, hurl that bucket as far as you can toward the church, and run like the dickens."

I waited until the most opportune moment, when I believed most of the men shooting at us were reloading, for I knew from the reports that most of them carried handguns.

"Now!" I shouted.

We threw our buckets into the air, then I grabbed Esmeralda by the hand and pulled her after me. We made a mad dash for the kitchen house, but I heard footsteps close behind us. One of our assailants was running after us across the courtyard, probably reloading as he ran. He surely would have a good shot at us in the moments we were held up by the closed door. But, as we approached the door, much to our surprise, it opened, seemingly by itself. Rounding the threshold, we were met by the menacing barrel of Quinn's Remington .50 caliber handgun. The detective had obviously heard the commotion and now stood by the door ready to cover us. As Esmeralda and I scrambled inside, I heard our pursuer shriek in terror as he too rounded the corner and realized he was looking down the barrel of a handheld artillery piece.

The next moment, Quinn's gun went off, the percussion only a foot or two from my ear and deafening me temporarily. I turned, expecting to see our pursuer missing a good portion of his head. Instead, I saw him writhing on the ground, shot through the leg. Quinn had only wounded him, albeit seriously. The detective now ejected the spent cartridge, filling the air with the smell of burnt gunpowder, produced another glimmering .50 caliber round and reloaded his weapon.

Then, he did nothing. He just stood there, holding his weapon on the struggling man, as if uncertain whether the man was sufficiently injured to no longer be a threat, clinging to his big city notions of limited use of force.

That was enough for me.

I snatched the Remington out of his hand, pointed it at the man on the ground and squeezed the trigger, putting a bullet through his chest. Tossing the weapon back to Quinn, I had the door shut before the man's body outside stopped twitching.

"When you shoot a man, make sure you shoot him dead!" I snapped at Quinn. "A wounded man can still fire a gun!"

Quinn appeared stunned by the cold way I had dispatched the prostrate man. Esmeralda and Domingo, too, looked at me as if they were in the presence of a monster, but there was little time to spare.

Instantly, my six-gun was thrust into my hand by Garcia and Esmeralda was given her shotgun. I was pleased to discover that the walls of this building were made of brick, and would protect us from most bullets. I was also happy to see that the house was devoid of windows, instead containing cross-shaped loopholes on each of the four walls. The Spanish constructors had certainly added them for the purpose of warding off Indian attacks, and they had known what they were doing. Together, the loopholes covered every possible approach to the house, offering an excellent view of the courtyard, as well as the twenty-yard clearing between the mission buildings and the waist-high wall surrounding the perimeter.

We each took up defensive positions, Quinn and I covering the long sides of the house, which contained two loopholes each, while Esmeralda and Garcia protected the single loophole on each of the other two sides.

It was darker inside the house that it was outside. The old man had had the sense to douse the lanterns. The moon was near full, bathing my field of vision with a pale blue that was just enough for me to pick out the buckskin coats and rawhide hats of our attackers running back and forth on the other side of the low, stone wall.

There was no doubting they were Martinique's men. As Quinn had warned, they had been dispatched here with all haste shortly after word of my release reached Martinique's ranch. They had probably discovered their two, hog-tied comrades as soon as they arrived. Thanks to my eastern friend's reluctance to administer western-style justice, the more cognizant of the two would have filled them in on what they were up against, and perhaps it was this knowledge that gave them the courage to make their next move.

As I watched the dark clearing, I was shocked to see several figures climb over the stone wall to my front and begin walking slowly toward the house.

"Here they come!" Quinn whispered, confirming they were approaching from his side as well. A nod from Esmeralda and her father at their own loopholes told me they could also see men approaching.

Martinique's men were either extremely well-paid, or just foolish, because they marched forward boldly, showing complete contempt for our ability to defend ourselves. Some held pistols, but most carried rifles. None bothered to take cover, as if the fight was already over, and all they needed to do now was smoke us out.

"Wait for my word!" I whispered to my companions.

I waited, and they waited. I waited until there were four men walking across the open ground before my loophole. When they reached a point halfway across, I decided it was time.

"Now!" I shouted.

All four of us opened fire at once, all four sides of the house discharging smoke at the same time, like a steam boiler bursting under pressure. I got off three good shots before the four men on my side hit the ground. At least one was on the ground because he was dead. He had dropped like a sack of potatoes. He had been the closest to me, and I had put a bullet in his heart. One of the others, I was sure I had winged, but I was unsure of the state of the other two. There were gravestones in the clearing, and my surviving assailants had scurried behind them for cover. I hoped my companions had been as successful. Whether they had been or not, a gun battle now ensued. Flashes from the muzzles of our enemy's guns flickered all around the house, and I could hear bullets striking the stone bricks near the loopholes, sending bits of dust and pebbles into the air.

A cacophony of gunfire hammered at our ears. The four of us kept up a steady fire, giving nearly as much as we received, and it wasn't long before the house was filled with swirling smoke and the acrid smell of gunpowder. Blasting loud above all the other guns, was Quinn's single-shot Remington – slow but steady, and deadly.

"Why?" cried old Garcia as he fired his Winchester rifle repeatedly. "Why do you keep coming?" He said between tears, clearly distraught at having to resort to such violence. But that was not the case with his daughter. Where her father was torn by a troubled conscience, and a troubled soul, Esmeralda fired and reloaded the shotgun as one who cared little for those on the receiving end. In fact, she seemed more invigorated with each successive shot,

169

sometimes blasting both barrels at once. I heard at least two men cry out after the savage discharges of her smoking barrels.

For my part, I reloaded at least three times, certain that at least two of my rounds had hit exposed arms, and one had grazed a scalp.

Bullets were flying at us, too, an incessant fusillade of lead that threatened to punch holes in the old brick walls. We had escaped injury, up until the moment I heard Garcia cry out in pain behind me. This happened just as the gunfire of our opponents was beginning to slacken. They were either withdrawing or had been told to cease fire.

"Hold your fire!" I said to the others.

Esmeralda took the opportunity to rush to her father's aid. All was still dark inside, so I did not see how severe the wound was.

"He's been hit in the chest!" she exclaimed, her voice frantic with worry.

"But I still live," came the weak reply from the old man, followed by a few coughs. "And I can still shoot."

As Esmeralda tended to her father, Quinn and I listened by our loopholes. We listened to see what transpired amongst our enemies. Soon, all gunfire ceased, and then, moments later, a solitary voice called out – a voice with a French accent.

"Hello in the house! Hello in the mission!" Martinique called.

"Keep a watch out at those loopholes." I whispered to my companions. "Shoot anything that moves." Then I raised my voice to converse with the man outside. "Go ahead! We're listening!"

"Is that you Mr. Jones?" he said. "Perhaps Mr. Quinn is with you."

Neither of us answered.

"I am ashamed of you Mr. Jones," Martinique continued in his snide manner. "Turning a place of peace and prayer into a place of such violence. The Holy Book says, *thou shall not kill*, Mr. Jones, but you have killed several of my men."

"If any of your men want to go to hell, Martinique," I replied. "We'll be glad to accommodate them. Just let them show themselves again."

"That would not be good for your soul, Mr. Jones. And it would be very expensive for me. You know what I seek, I believe, and it is not your death. Can we not reach a compromise? I want the priest's cross. More specifically, I want the map that it contained. Throw it out to me, and we will leave you in peace."

"I don't think so. The map doesn't belong to you, and what it leads to doesn't belong to you, either. This place is built like a fort, and we have plenty of ammunition. We can hold out for days – weeks, if necessary. So, you might as well gather up what's left of your boys and ride on out of here, before you lose any more."

"Maybe the others in there with you do not share your sentiments, Mr. Jones. I do not believe the map belongs to you, either, my friend. I extend my offer to all of those with you, as well. Can you all hear me?"

He was trying to set us against each other – divide and conquer, but such appeals would fall on deaf ears, if I had learned anything about my companions in the last few hours.

"You're a murderer, a liar, and a priest killer, Martinique," I snarled. "A coward, too, sending others to do your dirty work. Do you think us fools? You can't afford to let us go free."

I could hear Martinique laughing, and some of his boys joining in.

"You call me a killer, Mr. Jones?" he chuckled. "Isn't that the pot calling the kettle black? Come, now, we both know the truth. I wonder if you have shared it with those in there with you. Have you informed them of the evil deeds you have done in your life? Have you told the good Mister Domingo Garcia and his daughter what crimes you have committed?"

I did not turn to look at my companions. I would not have been able to see their faces in the dark, anyway. But I could feel their eyes on me, especially Esmeralda's. It felt as though I were the accused, watching a line of witnesses testify against me. Did this merely solidify her doubts? Could she ever trust me now? For the first time in my life, I felt ashamed of who I was. I wanted to ride out of here, leave this place, these people, the damned map, all behind me, forget them all and be on my way. But that feeling was overcome by a burning hatred welling up within me for that French bastard out there.

"Mister Martinique, this is Allen Quinn of the Pinkerton Agency," Quinn suddenly spoke up. "The U.S. marshal and several of his deputies will be here in two days, three tops. There will be a plethora of charges levied against you and your followers. You can't get to us in here – not without losing half your men. So, I would advise you, sir, if you know what's good for you, to collect what belongings you can and head for the Mexican border. If you stay, you and your men will surely face the hangman's noose."

Martinique laughed again. "Yes, Mister Quinn. That was quite a ruse you played on Sheriff Hobson. Rest assured, I am not so gullible. No telegram was sent, as you claimed. I have checked with the telegraph office. The marshal is not coming. No one is coming." He paused for a long moment, and I thought I heard him mumbling something to someone with him. I wondered if it was Julio. "I will extend my offer one more time," Martinique finally continued. "Surrender the map, and we will leave. Do not, and we will take it from you dead or alive."

"You have our answer, Martinique," Quinn said, with a bit more confidence than I had. Perhaps he was merely play-acting again. I wondered if he knew how precarious our situation truly was, as I did. For this makeshift fort of ours was not impregnable, especially not with a man like Julio advising Martinique. The range wars in New Mexico were nasty, sinister affairs, merciless and mean. Sometimes, the weapons employed went beyond flying lead and sharp blades. Julio would know exactly how to flush us out. I only hoped they had not the proper tools with which to do it.

CHAPTER XIII   A Father's Eyes

The gray light of dawn broke over the ridgeline to the east, bathing first the bell tower, and then the mission, in an orange glow. We had slept in shifts, one person at a time for one hour each, while the other two attended Garcia and watched for any excursion by Martinique's men. Luckily, no more attacks had come that night.

The old man was in a lot of pain, groaning more with each passing hour, and sometimes fighting for breath. The bullet was buried too deep to do anything about it without causing more harm. In the morning light, I could see that he was very pale, and I knew the only thing that could save him now was a skilled surgeon, but I kept this dismal conclusion to myself, not desiring to distress Esmeralda more than she needed to be. There was nothing that could be done about it. Imploring Martinique to send for a doctor would only give him another bargaining chip with which to tempt us – and he wanted us all dead, anyway.

Though we were all quite fatigued that morning, we were woken out of our stupor by the sound of a buckboard rattling up the road leading to the mission. Voices hailed the drivers. Our besiegers were up to something.

"Have they brought more men now?" Esmeralda asked, bleakly.

"Probably food and water for their own," Quinn commented. "They no doubt intend to starve us out."

Peering through the nearest loophole, I could just make out the wagon parked down beyond the gate in the outer wall. My view of it was somewhat obstructed by brush, but I could make out nearly a half dozen men unloading a large crate from the wagon. The crate was clearly heavy, and as I judged the dimensions and the size of it, I reluctantly deduced what it was, and bit my lip in frustration, because my worst fears had come true. This was not food, nor was it more ammunition. Martinique was a wealthy man, with many ventures in his portfolio. Mining was one of them.

"We have to get out of here!" I said to the others. "Now! They've brought dynamite!"

"They wouldn't dare use that on this holy ground!" Esmeralda exclaimed. "There are graves here."

"Shooting up the place doesn't seem to bother them, miss. I, for one, don't want to stick around to find out if they'll blow it up. We'll have to make a break for it. Is there a nearby gully, where we can maybe find some cover, once we're over the wall?"

Esmeralda did not answer, her eyes darting to her father. He would never manage such a dash in his condition. Quinn, now armed with Garcia's Winchester rifle, moved to the loophole looking out onto the courtyard.

"We could cut across the courtyard to the chapel. It's a long sprint across open ground, but I think we can make it."

"And then what?" I replied sharply. "Hide out there while they bring it down around us?"

"It was just an idea," Quinn said, offputtingly.

"A foolhardy one that would get us all killed!"

I took a deep breath, and made a slight apologetic nod to the detective. We were both frustrated more with the situation than with each other. He had said nothing all night about the fact that I had not told him about the map, but I knew it must have affected his trust in me. He had shown great restraint, and now I must.

"There...is...a way," the feeble voice of Garcia uttered.

But he was cut short by the sounds of crying goats and ringing bells outside.

"There are goats out there," Quinn exclaimed, looking through the loophole. "Lots of them. Milling about the graveyard."

"They've released them from our pens," Esmeralda said. "Why would they do that?"

"To distract us," I answered. "To provide them cover so they can get close to the house."

As I watched through one loophole, my view of the outer wall was periodically obstructed by a passing goat, but I saw movement on the other side. Two men were hunkering there, fiddling with something. Then I saw a trail of white smoke swirl into the air above them. One of them had struck a match, and I knew exactly what for. I held my gun near the window and waited for the first one to pop up. When he did, I was ready for him.

He was an unshaven ruffian, one of those I had seen in the saloon. He was hatless, and he had a sizzling stick of dynamite in his hand with an extremely short fuse. He was just in the middle of throwing when the bullet from my Peacemaker struck him in the cheek, but he had enough forward momentum to toss the dynamite clear of the wall and about half-way to the house. He then fell dead, slumped over the wall. In the instant before the explosion, I saw the shock on his companion's face as he realized the deadly stick was too close to him.

The blast was deafening. It shook the walls and the ground and knocked me back into the room, a cloud of thick dust blasting inside through the loopholes. The rafters above us seemed to shudder, but the sturdy house remained standing.

As we recovered from the concussion, and nearly coughed out our lungs for all the dust in the air, there was clearly disorder outside. Men were shouting at one another. I heard one man screaming at the top of his lungs in pain, presumably the wide-eyed man I had seen the moment before the blast.

"They will try again." I said, still wiping the dust form my eyes. "At some point, they will get through."

When I could finally see again, I was shocked to discover Garcia, on his feet, stumbling toward the loophole, Esmeralda's shotgun in his hands. He was clearly in a lot of pain, but he grunted his way into a position, propped up by a chair, such that he could see outside.

"Go!" He said to us, his sweat-streaked face caked with white dust. "Go now! Guide them, Esmeralda. You know the way. Go, before they come again."

Esmeralda rushed to his side, grabbing his arm, but he shoved her away.

"Go, daughter!" he said angrily, at first, but then his face softened and he smiled at her affectionately. When he spoke again it was in the loving voice of a devoted father.

"Go, my child. See that Father Perez's wishes are fulfilled. I love you."

There were tears in her eyes, but, after a long look at him, she complied.

"Come!" she said to Quinn and me, then opened the door to the underground passage, grabbed a lantern, and disappeared down the dark stairwell. Quinn followed her, but I paused, meeting eyes with old Garcia. He said nothing, but I could see a sincere appeal in his face, that I would watch out for his daughter and see her to safety. I nodded to him, then turned and rushed down the stairs.

We heard reports of the double-barreled shotgun behind us as Garcia fired at something outside, presumably more men with dynamite, and I began to think our decision to seek cover in the basement would be a fatal one.

"This is no good, Esmeralda!" I called ahead to her. "Any explosion that demolishes the house is likely to cave-in this room."

"We are not going to the room," was her only reply.

And she was right. No sooner had we reached the lower chamber, than she continued on through the dark passage in the opposite wall. This was of much cruder construction, and much smaller dimensions than the previous passage, and it descended even lower into the earth. We had been in the tunnel for only a few seconds, it seemed, when a massive sound like that of thunder sounded behind us, reverberated through the rock walls, and shook us off our feet. Dust and moisture trickled from the low ceiling, giving me the impression it might collapse at any moment. The half-rotted wooden supports along the tunnel offered little assurance.

Such a powerful blast must have come from several sticks of dynamite bound together, but one thing was evident, the house above us was demolished, and old Garcia had died in the blast.

Esmeralda wept quietly. Tears ran down her dirt-covered cheeks. Quinn and I both offered our sympathies, but she seemed not to hear them. Her grief had not broken her resolve. Rising, she brushed herself off, and continued deeper into the tunnel, holding the lantern out in front of her, as before, and we followed her.

CHAPTER XIV   The Padre's Tunnel

It seemed we groped our way through that dark tunnel for nearly a mile. From time to time, our boots stepped on relics from the past – an old lantern, pickaxes, a few shovels – all of them centuries old and undisturbed over the passage of time, as if their bearers had simply dropped them and had never returned to the cave. It was obvious this tunnel had not been used by the priests, or anyone for that matter, in quite some time.

"What is this place?" I asked Esmeralda.

"It is as old as the mission," she said, her tone still wrought with grief. "My father told me Juan de Castillo had it constructed in the event an Indian raid overran the mission."

"Where does it lead?"

She shrugged. "I do not know. I have never ventured this far."

The deeper we traveled, the more the tunnel's excavation deteriorated, the walls rougher, the ceiling lower, as if we were entering the unfinished portion of the tunnel. At one point, we were forced to crawl on our hands and knees to get past a spot where a boulder protruded into the passage. I began to doubt the tunnel led anywhere, but we had no choice but to press on.

We took hope from a wafting breeze coming from the darkness ahead. Just as it seemed the passage would narrow to the point we could go no farther, the tunnel soon became very spacious. The walls faded away into the blackness on both sides, and I could no longer see the ceiling. I had the strange sense that we were now outside and it was the middle of the night, but we were not outside, and it could hardly yet be noon. A constant drip echoed around us, and the air was muggy.

"My father told me of giant caverns down here," Esmeralda said, stretching out her arm to let the light of the lantern reach its maximum height.

I, too, had heard of the many vast caverns that lay beneath these mountains of the southwest, caverns so huge they defied the imagination, some containing bottomless chasms into which men and beasts have fallen, never to be heard from again.

All three of us gasped in awe as we saw the reflection of the light off the ceiling nearly forty feet above us and the giant chamber that lay before us. It was as if we had entered the auditorium of a big city theater. Several dozen stalagmites stood upon the floor of the cavern like silent, motionless patrons, patiently waiting for a show that would never begin. A path wound through this forest of cones, and from it we did not deviate. At one point, we came upon one of the aforementioned chasms. It lay just a few steps to the right of the path, a black void that swallowed up the light of the lantern.

"Remarkable!" Quinn commented in astonishment, whispering for some reason. "Is there no bottom to it?"

I picked up a small stone and tossed it over the edge. We counted to eleven before any sound of its impact echoed out of that pit. I wondered how many of those who had dug out the padre's tunnel made a misstep in the dark and took that same fatal plunge. How many broken skeletons lay in heaps at the bottom of that abyss?

With this ominous warning in mind, we proceeded at a much slower pace, keeping a wary eye out for any more such pits. The path guided us into another narrow tunnel, this one not as accommodating as the last, but filled with fresh air rich with the aroma of pine. This imbued in us a new vigor, which only strengthened when the tunnel assumed a steep upward slope. The soft dirt floor soon gave way to stones and pebbles, and eventually boulders. We weaved and climbed our way around every obstacle, until, finally, a tiny light appeared ahead of us. The light grew larger as we approached, tempting us with every step, filling us with both joy at the prospect of escaping these dark catacombs, and trepidation over what awaited us out there.

Were Martinique and his men waiting just outside with guns drawn?

At last, we reached the mouth of the cave, stepping out into the bright sunlight at the same time a small swarm of bats fluttered past us, stirred from their lair by our intrusion. The exit was just a gash in the land, a tear behind a clump of sagebrush. No one could have discovered it unless they had stumbled upon it. It was a foregone conclusion, our enemies had not found it.

Judging from the position of the sun, we had been in the cave for two or three hours, but the tunnel's tortuous nature left us uncertain whether we had placed some distance between us and the mission, or had merely walked in circles.

We heard voices in the distance, coming from beyond a slope to our front. On hands and knees, we peered over the summit and discovered, much to our surprise, that we were some two hundred yards away from the mission – or what was left of it.

I instantly put one hand over Esmeralda's mouth to keep her from crying out in anguish, for our position was slightly elevated and afforded a good view of the place – unfortunately, too good. The church and bell tower still stood, as did the perimeter wall, but the kitchen house, and the other outbuildings had been demolished. Of these, nothing remained but rubble.

But it was not the sight of the destruction that made Esmeralda wish to cry so miserably. Amid the still swirling dust, a dozen of Martinique's men sifted through the rubble, bandannas drawn over their mouths and noses. They had just removed a single body from the wreckage and had placed it unceremoniously amongst the tumbled gravestones. Mangled and streaked with blood, the body would have been unrecognizable were it not for the dust-covered clothes that unquestionably identified it as Garcia. The old man lay there, arms outstretched, one leg twisted in an unnatural fashion, his head rolled far to the side as if the neck was broken. He had probably died instantly, the moment the dynamite flattened the building, but that fact did little to temper Esmeralda's grief – or her anger. Despite this, she seemed to understand the potentially disastrous consequences of venting her grief, that any noise would surely give us away, so she buried her head in my chest, and beat her hands uselessly against my upper arms. I let her do this, feeling her tears through my shirt.

Strangely, all I could think about was the last time I had seen Garcia alive, when the old man had looked back at me with pleading eyes, that I might take care of his daughter, that I might protect her now that he no longer could.

As she wept quietly against my chest, her grief touched me. She had loved her father. There was an emptiness within her now, a hole in her heart that would be there from this moment on.

Would anyone grieve so for me when the bullet with my name on it finally caught up with me?

Perhaps it was at that moment that the gunfighter's spirit within me first began to diminish. I felt something I had not felt for a very long time – a desire to be needed, to be missed, to matter to someone.

"He died to save us," I said, feeling helpless to comfort her. "He died so that we could live. So that you could live. He was a good man."

She said nothing in reply but continued to hold onto me, and I did not miss the awkward diversion of Quinn's eyes, as if he believed we had embraced a bit too long.

We watched our adversaries from afar for several minutes, as we considered our next move. I could clearly make out Martinique's gray hair and Julio's flat-brimmed, Boss of the Plains hat. The two stood with hands on hips, watching their men dig through the devastation, probing every pile of rubble for the map.

"It's not going to take them long to figure out we aren't in that rubble." Quinn said.

I nodded and then gazed about a hundred yards to our left, where the road weaved through the pines. Martinique's men had tied off their horses there. We could see our own mounts there, as well. Martinique's men had evidently found them and had put them with their own. The rancher-baron was in such a feverish hurry to find the map that he now employed every one of his men in the search. None had been left behind to watch the mounts.

We made our way to the horses carefully, keeping the thick stands of trees between us and the mission as best we could so as not to be seen. Most of the horses had been tied to a long rope strung between two trees. The buckboard was parked there, too. Not far from it, lay a row of rigid corpses, the five men whom we had killed in the night. The dead men's coats had been removed and thrown over their faces to hide their features. Dark red patches marked their clothes where our bullets had hit, and the flies buzzed thickly around these ghastly wounds.

After collecting our own mounts, and picking one out for Esmeralda, we found a single-shot carbine on one of the other horses and also gave this to Esmeralda, along with whatever ammunition we could find.

"Go on ahead of me," I said to my two companions. "I'll join up with you later."

"What are you going to do?" Quinn asked from the saddle, looking at me quizzically. Beside him, Esmeralda eyed me with suspicion.

"I'm going to slow them up a bit," I answered, pulling my rifle from Carondelet's saddle. "Don't worry about me, just get Esmeralda and that map as far away from here as you can, and fast. Meet me at the Johnstone Livery Stables. Ride hard, and don't stop to play any tunes in Dougson. Martinique's liable to have men watching there. Least ways, that bastard of a bartender will be on the lookout."

Quinn shot me an annoyed look, but then nodded. Esmeralda's eyes softened a little, but I could see the jury was still out on her opinion of me. My companions then turned their horses around and trotted away. I waited for them to disappear down the road before crawling up a small rise topped with a flat stretch of sandstone from where I could once again see the mission.

Martinique and Julio stood with their backs to me, still watching the men as they searched the rubble. I could hear Martinique voicing his displeasure quite loudly whenever a document or scrap of paper was recovered and determined not to be the map. I could not hear what he said, but I could tell by the way he was scratching his chin and muttering to Julio, that he was already beginning to think we had somehow escaped, and that we had taken the map with us.

This was the moment – my only chance. I had this one opportunity to drastically improve our odds of escaping. It was cowardly. It was dishonorable. But I decided to take it.

It would be a long shot, one in which I would have to adjust my rear sight and elevate my rifle like an artillery piece, shooting my bullet with a high-trajectory in order to obtain the range, but I had killed from this distance before. It was far more likely, however, that I would wound whoever I hit. I knew it was likely that my prey would step right or left at the sound of the shot, which would probably reach his ears about half a second before my bullet struck – so I chose to aim at Julio's right shoulder.

I did not chose Martinique as my target because, should I only wound him, he could still delegate his dirty work from his bed. Julio was his de facto field commander. Julio was the one who coordinated the efforts of the other henchmen and kept them all in line. If I managed to kill or wound him, it would give us a decided advantage in our escape.

I did not wish to kill him in this way. After all, if there was any man in this backwards country I could relate to, any man whose past mirrored my own, it was Julio – but he was too good, and I would never have another shot like this one.

Judging the effect the wind would have on my bullet, I checked my aim one more time. The aim was good. The elevation was good.

I squeezed the trigger.

The next events happened so fast – all over the course of two, maybe three seconds – to this day, I can scarcely believe they happened.

My rifle recoiled, spewing a cloud of white smoke. It was a good shot. My trigger pull had been smooth and subtle, but as I waited for the bullet to travel the two hundred yards to its target, I saw Julio suddenly move to his left. He did not move of his own accord, he was pushed there, by someone standing on the other side of him, someone who now pointed one finger in my direction desperately trying to get Martinique's attention. The pointer had probably seen my muzzle smoke, or the glint of metal on my gun or on my person. Julio and Martinique each turned around to look where the man pointed, each one turning inward and unconsciously swinging their bodies away from the path of my bullet to let the pointing man stand between them.

The next moment, the pointing man was no longer pointing. His hand dropped to clutch his belly, red trickles seeping between the fingers. His black top-hat tumbled to the ground. There was no mistaking the slight, pot-bellied build of Sheriff Hobson. After informing his master of my release, he had accompanied him here, and now the pudgy law man had been pierced through the gut by my descending bullet. Even from this distance, I could hear him wail in agony and shock. He stared with wide eyes for several long seconds at the torrent of blood exuding from his gunshot belly. Then he dropped to his knees, and then, finally, face down in the dirt.

I myself was stunned that I had just shot dead the only thing close to a law man in these parts – albeit a corrupt one. I had taken a gamble in trying to kill Julio, and the only thing I had to show for it was a dead sheriff whose gun I would never have feared in a fight anyway. My dazedness lasted a bit too long, and I almost did not see Julio yank out his six-guns and send a rapid fusillade of shots in my direction. None of them came close to hitting me, of course. They were fired as he was scrambling for cover, the distance too great for any accuracy with a side-arm, even for Julio, but they were enough to spur me into action.

Now that Martinique and all his men were scampering for cover, I knew I must make my escape. I scooted back along the rock until I was hidden by the rise again, and then darted off toward the horses. With one swipe of my knife, I unhitched the entire herd. I then mounted Carondelet, fired my six-gun in the air a few times to set the others moving, and then galloped down the road through the mix of horses, trees, and dust, leaving behind a cursing lot of cowboys and gunmen.

CHAPTER XV   The Mogollon Rim

I met up with Quinn and Esmeralda at the Johnstone Livery Stable, as agreed. We would have preferred not to encounter anyone, but, as we entered the stables, we were met by Mister Johnstone himself. He greeted us suspiciously after seeing our dust covered clothing.

"Miss Esmeralda," he said, tipping his hat, obviously acquainted with our female companion. "What brings you out this way?"

"Nothing, in particular, Mister Johnstone," Esmeralda smiled brightly, hiding the grief she must have been feeling inside. "I am here with my friends. Just out for a day's ride."

Johnstone looked at me with distrustful eyes, though I had paid him a deposit two days ago for the boarding of my team. He looked at Quinn even more so, a stranger, whom he had never set eyes on.

"I've come to collect my mules, Mister Johnstone," I said. "I'll be settling up my account with you."

He looked at me sideways. "Didn't I hear, you got into some trouble in town yesterday? Trouble with the sheriff?"

"Yes, but that's all cleared up now," I said confidently, even though the three of us looked like we had just been sprung from prison. I gestured to Quinn. "Mister Quinn, here, is my lawyer. He took care of things. It was all a misunderstanding."

"Pleased to make your acquaintance, Mister Johnstone," Quinn said vibrantly, extending a hand.

Johnstone looked at the hand, but did not take it. He did not appear to believe a word of my story and returned his gaze to Esmeralda. "You alright, miss? These two aren't up to something, are they? Are they holding you against your will?"

"No, no." Esmeralda was quick to respond. "They are my friends, and friends of my father."

"You sure? You can run on into the house, if you like. Mrs. Johnstone would be right happy to see you."

"No, thank you. You are very kind. Please tell Mrs. Johnstone I regret not saying hello. I will call on her another time."

We put the packs on Don Carlos and Ulysses, and casually rode away with my team. Johnstone watched us from the stable door as we left. He stood there watching us, the thoughts running through his head evident on his grim face.

Once we were out of sight of the Johnstone property, we brought our mounts to a halt beside an abandoned corral where a flock of raven lighted on the rotting fenceposts. The crowing birds seemed to observe our every move, as if they, too, were employed by Martinique.

"What do we do now?" Quinn said. "We all saw the look in that old man's eyes. He's curious. It won't be long before he rides into town to check our story."

"Mister Johnstone is a good man," Esmeralda said. "He is not one of Martinique's men."

"He doesn't have to be. Once he starts asking around, Martinique will get wind of where we've been. He'll have a place to start looking, to try and guess our next move."

"What is our next move?" I asked.

"We retrieve the gold," Esmeralda replied fervently, patting the map in the pocket of her dress. "We must find it before that evil man does."

"But how can Martinique find it?" Quinn retorted. "He doesn't have the map."

"He may not have that," I said. "But he knows the gold is buried in some old ruins. That's why his so-called relic-seekers have been scouring the reservation for months. They may not know the gold is at Ciudadela, but if they overturn enough stones, they're bound to come across it."

196

Quinn shook his head. "Even if they do, we stand a much better chance if we ride straight to the territorial court at Prescott. There, we can legally secure the gold for my client."

"Your client?" Esmeralda asked stunned.

"Yes. The archbishop of Baltimore. We'll take it to the courts and file for an injunction stating that anything found in the old mission is the rightful property of the church, and should be delivered to the Archdiocese of Baltimore. Once the map is officially documented as belonging to the church, Mister Martinique won't be able to do much about it." After seeing the disbelieving look on Esmeralda's face, he added. "That's what Father Perez wanted, isn't it?"

"That is not what he wanted!" she exclaimed. "The gold does not belong to the church. It belongs to the native people of this land. Father Perez wished only for it to be returned to its true beneficiaries."

"I'm sure, once it is safe in the custody of the church, it will be dispositioned appropriately."

She looked at him blankly, as did I. There was little chance the church would ever give up the gold, once acquired. Quinn's expression indicated he well knew it. He smiled, silently conceding that point.

"My dear," he said, almost condescendingly. "It's not like this gold was taken out of the ground yesterday. Its true beneficiaries, as you call them, are long since dead and gone. If I'm not mistaken, the tribes around here were nomadic savages at that time, roaming from here to Mexico. There's no guarantee they had any relation to those who toiled in Castillo's mine."

"You men are all the same," she said scathingly. "You treat Indians as a single group. You mete out punishment to peaceful and hostile tribes, alike. Then, when it pleases you – or rather, when it is to your advantage – you treat them as individual tribes and clans. Shameful!"

"In any event, Miss Esmeralda." Quinn appeared to be growing annoyed with her now. "It is best for the territorial court to decide. Prescott is our best option, for the simple fact that we must report your father's murder, and the rest of Martinique's misdeeds. That man must be arrested. I would think you, more than anyone, would wish to see him dancing at the end of a rope."

"You do not realize his influence here," she sighed. "He has friends in the territorial legislature. Many of the judges and officials are his associates. He can produce witnesses at will. Do you think our word will carry any weight? He will never spend one day in jail, let alone be charged with the murder of my father and the priests. Believe me, he is too clever for that. His brute, the one they call Julio, gunned down a man on the streets of Dougson in broad daylight, murdered him in cold blood. Many people saw it happen, but when the U.S. marshal came to investigate, no witnesses could be found. No one came forward. All around here know what happens if you cross Martinique."

"He will answer to the law, madam."

She looked at him appallingly. "Have you heard nothing I have said, Mister Quinn? If you try to put the law after Martinique, it is very likely you will end up hanged yourself. What you suggest is foolishness. We must find the gold! That is the only hope for justice – to deprive that evil man of the only thing he cares about. We must!"

"Begging your pardon, miss," Quinn said. "But you and your father were merely employed by the church. You have no stake in this. I have allowed you to keep hold of that map, but only out of respect for your poor father and his sacrifice. I hesitate to be so blunt, but let me be very clear on this point. The map belongs to my client." He looked at me for support. "Jones, talk some sense into her."

A wistful gaze from Esmeralda carried with it hope that I would see things her way. In the few hours I had known her, I had detected a knowledge of the western frontier commiserate with my own. She was right. This was not sophisticated Baltimore with its pedigreed lawyers and principled courts. Out here, law and justice had different meanings and different forms.

"You're wrong, Quinn," I replied, much to the detective's surprise. "In these parts, possession is ownership. Out west, many of those who sit the bench, or wear a badge, were themselves once on the wrong side of the law. I've seen bad ones. I've seen good ones. I've never seen any that didn't owe their position to someone with a lot of power. You surrender that map to any court around here and, chances are, someone there will be sympathetic to Martinique and let him get his hands on it."

"What, then? We just dig it up and carry it off ourselves, like a band of pirates?"

"Yes," Esmeralda answered first. "We carry it to another place, a place where Martinique cannot find it. When the gold is safely hidden, then we may concern ourselves with who it belongs to."

"I see no other choice," I concurred.

Quinn appeared slightly annoyed at my siding with Esmeralda, but she gave me an appreciative nod. I smiled back to her, trying hard not to display the wave of guilt flooding over me, for I had not sided with her out of any desire to uphold the wishes of her father or the old priest. I had my own reasons. I wanted the gold. Though I felt a growing affection for Esmeralda, the gold was indeed the only reason I was here.

Every man who comes out west, comes for a reason. This had been mine, all those years ago, after the war. To start over, and make my own fortune. To have my own spread, and never have to beg, borrow, steal, or give to any other man. To owe nothing and be owed nothing. To just be. To watch the sun rise and set over land that was my own, and that no one would ever take from me. This was finally my chance to have that dream, and I was not about to squander it.

We reached the base of the five-hundred-foot cliffs that separated the plateau from the foothills. The craggy escarpment far above looked down menacingly upon us, as if up there were another world, untamed by man, and, in many ways, this was true. Once upon the plateau, we would have to watch for Indians as well as any of Martinique's men whom we assumed would be hot on our trail. We paused only to stare at the massive formations above us before dismounting and beginning the long ascent up the winding trail.

The afternoon thunderstorms hung upon the cliffs as if to conceal their majesty from the valley below. It made me suddenly recall one of the books I read in my youth, Frankenstein. Though I had never been to Europe, it seemed a short stretch that those cliffs might have been transplanted from the Alps, and that Montanvert's summit and Doctor Frankenstein's creature might be hidden in those angry clouds. It goes without saying, I chose not to share these thoughts with my companions.

It was a long ascent, one switchback after another, at the end of each one the cliff seemingly no closer than before. The roiling clouds, however, were closer than ever, their discharging bolts filling the air with static electricity. At the beginning of our ascent, I had kept my eyes on the forested valley below, looking for any sign of our pursuers on the road that wound in and out of the thick woods, but as we drew closer to the clouds, my concern shifted to that of nature and all her hazards.

The thunderstorms of these lands were dazzling to behold, a ballet of spectral energy amongst towering columns of cumulus. Oftentimes I would stop to watch them from afar, amazed at Our Maker's hand and His almighty power. But being under one of these terrible, violent, unrelenting storms was another thing entirely.

The flashes of lightning lit up the trail and the cliffs above us brighter than the brightest day. An instant later, a cacophony of thunder clapped all around us, frightening the mules, shaking the ground and reverberating through the trees. Each strike left a man feeling fragile, helpless, as if he lay upon the anvil of God, spared once but just as easily struck down at the next bolt.

I could see the trepidation on Quinn's face as we climbed closer to the sources of this menace. Had we not been fleeing under the threat of armed pursuers, I would have demanded we seek cover, for I had on two occasions witnessed the lethal power of these bolts – once, in an open field, when a calf was struck down not twenty paces from me; the other time, on the Mississippi, during the war, when lightning struck our riverboat, instantly killing a hand who had been working on the open deck with a fender pole. Between rebel artillery shells and boiler explosions, I saw much horrible death and destruction on that river. I pulled more bodies from the muddy waters than I'd like to count. But no image stuck with me longer than the sight of that lightning-struck man, splayed on the deck, his hair singed, and his ears entirely missing, for they had been blown clean off.

I had been in many gunfights, but nothing got my nerves jumping more than close lightning. There was something about that manner of death that unsettled me then, and still unsettles me to this day. The evidence of its terrible wrath was visible along the path. One could scarcely find a spot from which a craggily, hollowed out, lightning-struck tree was not visible, standing bare against the sky. Like sacrificial lambs, they had died that the other trees might live, for this forest depended on these powerful, roaming storms to survive the hot months.

It began to rain, the water coming down in torrents, a hard, pelting rain, icy and nearly hail. The trail was steep, and our ascent was agonizingly slow. I had spent much of the last few years in the mountain country and counted myself in good condition for such a climb, but even I was severely winded.

As we climbed higher into the cloud bank, the forested valley floor below us grew more obscure, and finally disappeared altogether. We exchanged unsettling glances, each of us understanding, with the trail hidden, there was no way for us to know if Martinique and his men were hot on our trail, pursuing us on fresh mounts, or if they had lost our trail altogether.

It was near dark when we finally gained the rim. The storm had moved off into the valley below, a bubbling dark mass accentuated by the luminosity of periodic flashes.

"Let's pull them off the trail a few hundred yards," I said, guiding Carondelet off into the trees.

"Didn't you say the ruins were thirty miles north of here?" Quinn asked puzzlingly, though Esmeralda seemed to understand my intent.

I motioned to the horses. "They need a rest. If we don't rest them, they won't be worth a damn to us if we come across Martinique's men," I paused, and then added, "Or Apaches."

Quinn's face drew suddenly serious. That thought had clearly not occurred to him. He began to study the forest around us, as if a painted warrior might spring from the ground and attack him at any moment. Those who dwelt in the West long enough knew well to respect and fear the skills of the Apache. Most folks, if they hadn't experienced an attack first hand, knew someone who had. If westerners feared the Apache, easterners held the fierce warriors in an almost mystical reverence, having read in the Sunday paper over tea and coffee how an outpost was attacked, or a wagon train of wayward pioneers was captured and tortured, their children kidnapped and raised to become savages. Most of those stories were not true, but enough were to make the legend stick, and tease the imagination.

Though we were exhausted, cold, and wet, we did not make a proper camp that night. We found a dense glade that would conceal us well, and unpacked our mounts that they might have some relief. It was a most uncomfortable night, without a fire, the wet clothes on our backs chilling us enough to set our teeth chattering. Despite this discomfort, my companions held up better than I had expected. Esmeralda rested in silence, her back against a tree, never once uttering a single word of complaint, like an unshakable, veteran cattle driver. Quinn stayed silent, too, but for different reasons I suspect. My comment about the Apaches had set his imagination running wild, and he sat up all night holding the Winchester in one hand, and his Remington in the other.

CHAPTER XVI   The High Desert

We set out the next morning at first light. The evening thunderstorms had all but evaporated, leaving a clear blue sky above us and damp mulch beneath our horses' hooves. Ever mindful of the threat of pursuit, we moved at a fast pace, resting the horses and my mules less frequently than I would have liked, though we had little other choice. Still, even after hours of riding, we had not seen or heard any parties behind us.

"Is it possible they have not followed us?" Esmeralda asked hopefully.

"It may be, miss," Quinn commented with equal optimism.

Though my companions were beginning to breathe easier, I did not. For I knew there were other ways to ascend the rim, aside from the wagon road we had used. There were steep passes, well away from the trodden paths, often used by Indians. It was just a year ago that the renegade Apache Na-tio-tish, after a brief period spent terrorizing the towns and settlements along the Tonto Basin, used one of these passages in an attempt to escape the pursuing U.S. cavalry. It was possible Martinique and his men had used one of these paths. If that was the case, and if he had a good scout with him, he might yet find our trail. Or, if Johnstone had blathered in town about seeing us, then Martinique might have already guessed which ruins we were headed to, and might very well beat us to Ciudadela. With these possibilities in mind, I kept a wary eye out both ahead and behind us as we continued our journey north.

By late morning, the forest began to thin, allowing more of the sun's rays past the shady canopy above us. Eventually, the trees diminished entirely, letting us out onto a vast high desert plain sparsely dotted with low hills and tall, pyramid-like mounds, some of which I knew were long extinct volcanoes. When traveling north or south in the Arizona Territory, the landscape often changed drastically in the course of only a few dozen miles.

"This isn't wise, being out in the open like this," Quinn commented. "We can be seen for twenty miles in every direction."

He was right. I didn't like it either, but we had no choice. There was no inconspicuous way to reach the Ciudadela ruins. We tried our best to stick to the gullies and washes, minimizing our time spent on the higher ground, and trusting to the fact that Martinique's party would be much larger than ours, and thus we had a better chance of sighting them first.

It was on the summit of one of those hazardous hills that we believed our worst fears had come true, when we spied a row of white dots on the distant horizon ahead. Believing it to be Martinique and his men, or the teepees of some Apache band, we immediately dismounted and drew our horses back behind the hill to avoid being seen. But, after a few moments spent cursing in frustration, we got the notion to crawl back to the summit on our bellies to get a better look.

"Soldiers," Esmeralda concluded, her eyes being better than mine, and much better than the bespectacled detective's.

After a long minute of squinting, I saw that she was correct. The distant white dots were unquestionably rectangular army tents, arranged in neat rows. Upon further study, I saw horses bivouacked together, and a perimeter of sentries, behind which men in blue went about the daily camp routines of a troop on patrol. We counted about forty soldiers. The camp appeared to be temporary as if the troops did not intend to remain more than a few nights. I assumed this troop belonged to the major I had met in the Two Players saloon.

Were they still looking for artifact hunters, or were they, too, in the employ of Martinique? Perhaps they had been dispatched here to search for three dangerous outlaws – two men and one woman – wanted by the local law enforcement establishment.

Not knowing their intentions or their allegiance, we decided to give them a wide berth. It slowed us considerably, and consumed the better part of the day, but we carefully skirted around the cavalry encampment, making a large semicircle across the plain, before continuing our journey north.

The sun was just setting when the army tents disappeared over the horizon behind us. As the light diminished, the evening winds picked up, chilling us to the bone, for our clothes were still damp from the day before. We decided to make camp in a small gully where we could make a fire without being seen.

I had two changes of clothing, kept dry inside my canvas packs. One of these, I shared with Quinn, and the other I donned myself, but only after Esmeralda refused them.

"Those are too big for me," she said firmly. Despite being cold and wet, despite being out in the middle of nowhere, she made it very clear she did not wish to dress like a man. "I will dry my own clothes by the fire."

Quinn and I stood there gaping as she stepped behind a sage and proceeded to undress. At the first glimpses of her supple, bare shoulders glowing in the firelight, our mouths must have dropped open, because she shot us an annoyed look.

"Do you have nothing better to do?" she said abruptly, stirring us from our stupor.

"Yes, ma'am," I stuttered, then pulled the dazed Quinn along to follow me.

Quinn and I left the warmth of the campfire and occupied ourselves with tending to the animals, grooming them, and checking them for injuries from the day's journey, all the while trying hard not to think too much about what Esmeralda would have looked like had that sagebrush not been in the way.

I gave Carondelet a few oats by hand. His large mouth gobbled them up, his wet tongue and teeth barely touching me. He was clearly appreciative, and I patted his powerful neck. Quinn seemed amused that I would nurture Carondelet so, but I ignored him and continued to indulge my faithful friend of many trails. What did a city-slicker understand about the bond between a man and his horse, anyway?

"Carondelet," he said, with a chuckle. "Where did you ever come up with a name like that? Seems like something shorter would be easier – Dusty, or Sancho, or Lightfoot, perhaps. What the hell does *Carondelet* mean, anyway?"

"This is no common horse, my friend," I replied, rubbing my horse's black mane. "He rates more than a common name. He's named after an ironclad I served on during the war."

Quinn laughed. "Now that's something I simply cannot picture. You, a sailor."

"A riverboat man is not a sailor. He is a different breed altogether."

"On that point, I will not dispute you."

"What about you?" I said. "Where did you serve during the war."

"I did not," Quinn said, after a long sigh.

"Oh."

"I was sixteen when the war ended. Too young to have taken part. Too young to bear the honors and distinction of a veteran, yet old enough, it seems, to be hounded by that question until the end of my days – doomed to endure the doubting glances and curious whispers."

"I meant no unkindness. I believe your actions at the mission prove your valor."

He laughed again. "Now isn't that just my luck. The only witnesses to my bravery are a bunch of outlaws and brigands."

"There's me," I replied. But after he shot me a questioning glance that suggested he had lingering misgivings about my own standing with the law, and the fact that I had kept the existence of the map a secret from him, I conceded. "Well, in any event, there is the girl."

"Indeed," he said, musingly looking back in the direction of the campfire. "There is the girl."

By the time we returned to the campfire, Esmeralda's clothes were hung on a scraggly tree and she was wrapped in one of my dry blankets. I watched her endless eyes gaze into the fire. She was beautiful in every way, and I began to imagine things I knew I had better not, so I averted my eyes. My mother instilled in me a few redeeming qualities, at least. I was a gunfighter and, yes, I was a killer, but I'll be damned if I ever considered myself anything less than a gentleman.

Quinn and I agreed to take turns at the watch, Quinn volunteering to take the first interval, though his disquieted nature from the previous evening was rapidly returning as the night grew darker. The howls of wolves and coyotes traveled across the prairie. They were far away, but Quinn appeared convinced that each one was an Apache.

Before I drifted off to sleep, I could not help but cast a glance at Esmeralda. Her bedroll was only a few paces from mine. She had already fallen asleep, turned away from me and lying on her side. The blanket had slid down just enough to expose her bare shoulders. The sight of her smooth skin in the pale moonlight, not to mention the way in which the gray wool conformed to the curve of her hip, played games with my senses. Eventually, I fell asleep, dreaming of what else lay hidden beneath that blanket. It was a sublime restful moment, but it did not last long.

It seemed I had only slept a few minutes when my delightful repose was abruptly cut short by a hand roughly shaking me awake. I opened my eyes to see Quinn above me, his Remington in one hand, his eyes looking nervously off into the darkness.

"I heard something," he whispered urgently.

I rose quickly, drawing my Peacemaker, and not bothering to don my boots. Our fire had dwindled to just a few red coals, leaving most of the camp in the dark. I listened intently but heard nothing apart from the distant calls of wildlife.

"What was it?" I asked. "What did you hear?"

He pointed off to a clump of sagebrush. "Over there. I heard the call of a bird. It was close. Right behind me!"

I could see nothing beyond the brush, only darkness, but the horses and mules appeared somewhat skittish.

"I'll take the watch," I said. "Try to get some sleep. "

"Sleep? After that? Not likely."

Quinn retired to his bedroll, still scanning his surroundings, but his fatigue eventually won out over his anxiety. After a few tosses and turns, he was snoring loudly in time with the crickets. He would have had a harder time getting to sleep had I told him the real reason I had taken the watch early.

I thought it very likely we were being watched.

That Quinn had heard something, I did not doubt. The gully we inhabited was simply too quiet. There was a distinct silence that seemed unnatural, as if an entire section of the insect chorus had stopped singing. Whether the intruder was creature or man, I could not tell. If man, then it was just one or two men. Otherwise, they would have attacked us by now – assuming they meant us harm.

Either way, I intended to find out.

There is an old trick often used by Indians. They lure their enemies with seemingly harmless bait, something perceived to be easy prey, something too good to pass up. A few wickiups with a handful of squaws and children milling about are tempting targets to a band of scalp-hunters. When the over-confident hunters carelessly swoop in for the kill, they find themselves ambushed by armed braves lying in wait. Often it is the scalp-hunter who ends up missing his scalp.

I decided I would offer a similar trap to our silent visitor. Throwing another block of juniper on the fire, I let the flames flicker back to life. After an ostentatious yawn, I leaned back on my saddle, tipped my hat down over my eyes, and pretended to fall asleep.

Our intruder was now presented with an unguarded camp containing three slumbering people – one of them a woman. He would at least try to get a closer look. The temptation would be too great. Esmeralda and Quinn might not have approved of me using them as bait, but they would not understand. If this intruder meant us harm, this was our best chance of thwarting it.

Nothing happened for quite some time. I waited, and waited, for at least an hour, the crackling fire and Quinn's snoring nearly lulling me back to sleep. Then, I heard it. First, a call like that of a nightingale, very close, then rustling in the brush to my left. I instantly stirred back to full alertness, but I did not move.

Beyond the brim of my hat, I saw a shadow emerge from the darkness, moving noiselessly on bare feet. The light of the fire soon revealed a crown of straight shoulder-length hair, held in place by a headband. It was an Apache, for sure. Gingerly, but swiftly, he crept through our camp, tip-toeing directly toward the slumbering Esmeralda. It seemed she was his only purpose.

The Peacemaker was in my hand. I could have killed him then and there, but I assumed he had a compatriot watching to ensure I did not wake up. I had only a moment to deduce the intruder's intentions, and my only conclusion was that he desired Esmeralda for himself, and wished to kidnap her as a prize. I had only a second to ponder this before I saw the moonlight reflect off something in the Indian's hand.

He held a knife.

"Stop!" I shouted, firing my weapon once into the air, the cacophony instantly jolting both of my companions awake.

The report of the gun had startled the Indian. He stood there for a moment, examining himself as if he expected to have been hit. When he realized he wasn't, he turned to look in my direction. I saw his sweat-streaked face in the glimmer of the dwindling fire. Then he was gone, padding away through the brush.

I had only seen his face for an instant, but that was enough to recognize the face I had once seen from closer than I preferred. It had been the face of Long Musket, the young Apache I had fought on the rim a few days ago. A rustling behind me told me he had a companion, and that both had departed at a sprint. There was little chance of catching them, and I did not wish to ride them down.

By the time Quinn and Esmeralda had the wherewithal to know what was going on, the Apaches were gone.

"Who were they?" Quinn said from one knee, holding his Remington at the ready.

"Apaches," I replied simply.

"How can you be sure?"

"I've run into this band before." They both looked back at me in surprise. "They were after you, miss. I don't know why. It's been a long time since I've heard of Apaches carrying anyone off."

She looked back at me with her best display of courage, but I could tell the incident had ruffled her to the core. The thought of being carried off by Indian warriors was the nightmare of every woman living in the West. The stories were still fresh in the minds of most in this country, about the depravities and inhuman suffering visited upon women captured by certain warrior bands during the wars of decades past. Of course, there were bad apples in every bunch. There were despicable bastards on both sides of any war. I witnessed many unspeakable acts during the war between the states, some committed against civilians, some against women and children, some against slaves. These things were seldom recorded. Likewise, during the bloody Indian wars, atrocities were committed by bad apples on both sides.

Perhaps this Long Musket was simply that – a bad apple. If that were the case, then certainly the older Apache I had met that day, Red Vest, would be considered a good apple, a man with a cool head, and a clear thinker. Then I began to wonder, if Long Musket was here, on this prairie, was it possible that Red Vest was here as well, along with my other Apache friends?

I could not decide whether that thought gave me comfort or further apprehension, as my companions reluctantly went back to sleep, and I once again assumed the watch.

CHAPTER XVII   Ciudadela

The next morning, we saw no sign of our late-night visitors, aside from a few footprints in the sand. Though Esmeralda seemed to have recovered from the alarming incident, Quinn was still quite disturbed by it. Despite his angst, he insisted on returning my more practical clothes and donning his own wool suit again, which was now dry, as were Esmeralda's clothes. The suit seemed to give him comfort, as if it were the only thing he had to remind him that he came from a civilized land far away.

We continued our journey across the grassy plain as the sun followed its course in the sky. We could have been the last three humans on earth, the plain was so devoid of animal life. Dust devils in the distance often deceived us into thinking someone was on our trail, but the swirling clouds of dust invariably faded into the blue sky.

Around noon, another dazzling sight came into view, a ribbon of color spanning the northern horizon from one end to the other, as if The Almighty had dipped a great brush in orange and red paints and then drew a thick line across the landscape.

"*El Desierto Pintado*," Esmeralda said, as all three of us gazed in awe.

That was the name given it by Coronado, the conquistador who travelled this way three centuries ago on his search for the Seven Cities of Cibola. No matter how many times I saw it, the Painted Desert always looked out of place to me, as though it belonged on another continent, or another world, like it had been stitched onto the canvas of the Colorado Plateau. It marked the beginning of the Navajo lands, bounded by their four sacred mountains, restored to the tribe after the tragedy of the Long Walk.

The plain grew sparser the further we went. The sage and juniper that had stood infrequently among the tall grass were replaced by jagged boulders of lava rock. It had been many years since I had traversed this plain, and one hill was starting to look like another. I was beginning to have doubts about my own guidance as the sun descended in the western sky, and was about to suggest we turn back, when Esmeralda called out.

"There!" she said, pointing to a distant mound. "There it is!"

Her eyes were indeed better than mine. It was not until we travelled a few miles closer that I could finally make out the rocky formation standing atop the mound like a cylindrical pedestal, one side bathed in the light of the late afternoon sun, the other side a dark shadow. We were closer still before I discerned the broken walls and collapsed structures amid the piles of stones at its base.

"For the love of..." Quinn gasped in wide-eyed amazement. "I've never seen the like! It looks like a ruined castle!"

"That is Ciudadela," I said.

The Ciudadela ruins consisted of a fortress, of sorts, overlooking a small village. Before us, stood a gentle slope rising out of the plains up to the base of a fifty-foot-high rocky escarpment – the remains of some cataclysmic upheaval or volcanic event. The escarpment was perhaps fifty yards across, with a flat top, and sharp cliffs dropping off at its fringe. From a distance, the giant rock formation resembled a medieval castle, or citadel, standing atop a mound – hence its name. It was mostly natural, except for a rock wall that lined its edge. The citadel presented sheer drops on all sides, except in one place on the east side, where its shadow now fell. There, the descent was more gradual, as if, thousands of years ago, one side of the rock had collapsed under its own weight forming a natural ramp to the top. Upon this slope stood the ruins of the village, some three or four dozen structures in various states of decay. Each one was constructed of flat stones and mortar crafted into uniform walls nearly two feet thick. It was impossible to ascertain the exact dimensions of the original buildings since time and neglect had toppled most of them – only a handful stood more than a few feet high – but it was not too difficult to imagine what the village must have looked like in its heyday.

As we approached the ruins, we rode past an elliptical pit partially filled with rocks. It was as large as a tennis court and uniform on all sides. Who knew what the ancient inhabitants once did here? Was it some kind of auditorium, or perhaps a gladiatorial arena where warrior faced off against warrior to the death? Or did it have a more sinister purpose, like sacrificing animals, or maybe humans? Surely, we could only guess at its purpose, as with everything else we encountered here. One thing, however, was abundantly clear. An intelligent people once thrived here, a people with their own songs, their own fears, and their own dreams. They made their home in the middle of this high, barren desert for who knows what reason, and for who knows how many centuries. Children laughed and played in these streets. Men and women fell in love and struggled to provide. Like any other people, they worried about the future, and spoke fondly of the past. As dismal as it seemed to us, it had been a sanctuary to them. Whenever necessity took them to other lands, they would have missed it, even yearned for it, and the citadel's black rocks poking above the plain would have been a welcome sight on their return.

Now, they were gone forever. These rocks, once warmed by a hundred cooking fires, felt only the bitter wind now. The ancient ones had vanished, leaving behind only this assortment of stone heaps overgrown with prairie grass as evidence they had ever existed.

We weaved through the alleyways formed by the ruins, a maze of half-standing walls, some connected, some not, all forming square or rectangular rooms open to the sky, the roofs having long since rotted away. We started up the ramp to the citadel. When the terrain became too steep, we dismounted and continued on foot, bringing our rifles with us. The thin air made us light-headed as we climbed up the narrowing path, but, when we reached the summit, we forgot all about our fatigue. Once more, we gasped in amazement. The vast landscape all around us seemed to stretch to the ends of the earth. To the west, the twelve-thousand-foot San Francisco Peaks jutted above the horizon. The sun was just beginning to set behind them. To the north, the Painted Desert, bathed in the sun's last rays, was grander and more dazzling than before. To the east and south, the endless grassy plain was already masked in shadow, and growing darker as the sun sank behind the mountains. As breathtaking as the view was, the fading light spoiled any chance of spying anyone following our trail – if indeed anyone was pursuing us at all.

"This truly is a citadel," Quinn said, pointing to the low rock wall that wrapped around the escarpment. In many places, the wall stood so close to the edge that one step beyond it would result in a fifty-foot drop. "Do you suppose the original inhabitants ever used it for defense?"

I shrugged. "I've seen my share of fortifications, especially during the war. The rebels had a lot of them along the Mississippi and the Tennessee. They built them on bluffs overlooking long stretches of water, so that no boat could get close without running a devastating gauntlet of fire. I'd say this spot was chosen for the same reason. No enemy would stand a chance sneaking up on this place – unless they did so at night."

Our eyes met, each sharing the same thoughts. If Martinique's men were indeed out there on the plain, they might very well sneak up on us in the dark. There was little we could do about it. They might approach from any

225

direction. Our best bet was to find the gold and get out of here as fast as we could.

I was about to ask Esmeralda to break out the map, when I noticed it was already in her hands. She stood near the edge alternately studying the map and the village below. Then, quite suddenly, she folded up the map and began marching back down the path.

"Where are you going?" I called after her as Quinn and I followed. "Wait!"

"My father spoke of a creek that was nearly dry," she said, not breaking her stride. "There is a dry gully down there, running past the village. That has to be it! According to the map, the cave is at the source of the creek."

After retrieving a lantern from my packs, we descended into the gully Esmeralda had seen from above. It was bone dry now, but its banks were lined with trees and green brush indicating it had flowed in the not too distant past. We did not have to follow its winding course for very long before it disappeared into a clump of brush at the base of the citadel, on the opposite side from which we had approached. Drawing the foliage aside, we found the cave just where the map said it would be.

I struck a match and lit the lantern that we might bet a better look at it in the diminishing light.

"Well, I'll say one thing for him," muttered Quinn, as we all stared into the dark cavity. "Father Perez certainly knew his maps."

The cave may have been a natural formation at one time, but its smooth edges indicated the ancient ones had fashioned it for their own use. We ducked inside and discovered it was more of a cavern than a tunnel, a large circular room, where twenty or so people might sit comfortably while a flash flood raged outside. The walls were covered with the soot of age-old campfires and pictographs of every kind, all of them meaningless to us. A sunken patch of mud on the ground revealed where the spring had once bubbled out of the earth. Tracks of various animals were impressed into the dry ground surrounding it. A pile of debris in one corner turned out to be nothing more than a collection of animal bones.

As the light of my lantern touched every corner of the cavern, we began to look at each other in confusion. This was without a doubt the cave indicated on Father Perez's map, but it was empty. There was no horde of gold here.

"Well, where the hell is it?" Quinn said, visibly disappointed.

"It has to be here," Esmeralda said. "It must be. My father would not lie."

"Maybe someone looting the ruins came across it," I suggested. "Your father said he and the priests hid it here some years ago. I'm sure someone has visited these ruins since then, either relic hunters, or Indians."

"Maybe Martinique's men beat us to it!" Quinn said, picked up a stone and hurling it out of frustration.

The stone struck the sloping ceiling on the far side of the cave and rebounded straight down, but when it hit the ground, an unexpected sound reached our ears. The stone was about the size of a man's palm, heavy enough that its impact with the floor of the cave should have resulted in a dull thud, but that is not what we heard. We heard a hollow reverberation, as if the stone had landed on top of a wooden plank. Upon closer inspection, and some digging with our hands, we discovered that the powdery dirt where the stone had landed was only a few inches thick. Beneath it was a large sheet of canvas which we pulled up to reveal a floor of loose wooden planks, covering an area about the size of a buckboard. After exchanging looks of exhilaration and trepidation with my companions, I moved two of the planks aside revealing a dark cavity beneath. Holding the lantern to the opening, all three of us peered inside. There, several feet below, the glimmering sheen of metal peeked back at us from the void, as if ashamed that we had found it.

"Montezuma, turn over in your grave!" Quinn exclaimed.

Esmeralda put a hand to her chest as if unable to breathe.

The next moments were a blur. I am not sure what happened, other than that the gold fever had taken hold of each of us, because within a matter of seconds we had every plank tossed aside and had leapt into the shallow pit to touch and feel the precious treasure and gaze upon it with eyes of avarice. Then we were all suddenly laughing and beaming with delight, all inhibitions gone for those few moments. I cannot explain the euphoria that had come over us, but I had never seen so much gold in all my life. There were upwards of two hundred gold ingots in that pit, all stacked one upon the other in neat rows, all unmarked, as might be expected of gold stolen from an illegal mining operation.

"There must be four hundred thousand dollars in gold here!" Quinn announced in ecstatic disbelief.

Even Esmeralda giggled like a schoolgirl, as if she had harbored some uncertainty about her father's stories until now.

I, too, had not been a true believer until that moment, but my gold-driven state of ecstasy did not last quite so

229

long as that of my companions. For, in my mind, I was already devising some plan as to how I might make off with it all and leave these two behind.

Of course, I didn't wish any harm to come to them. I would, at the very least, leave them their horses and plenty of provisions, but I was determined to seize most of this treasure for myself. The means for making all my dreams come true was now gleaming before my face, and I was not about to let it get away.

The deal I was about to present to my companions was simple, and quite reasonable, really. There was a lot of gold here. Even if we emptied all our packs and filled them to the brim with gold bars, we could not take all of it. I would propose we divide up the gold between us. Each could carry away all the gold he or she could manage. My companions could load down their horses and go about their merry way, and give their portion of the treasure to Indians, or priests, or archbishops in Baltimore, or to whomever they wished. Likewise, I would ditch my existing cargo and load up Don Carlos and Ulysses with my portion – admittedly, the lion's share – and ride off in the opposite direction.

It seemed a perfectly sensible proposal to me. Quinn had earlier argued with Esmeralda that the map belonged to his client. Well, the mules belonged to me. Thus, everything on them belonged to me. We would each take our share of the gold and go our separate ways. They would have to go along with it. The only thing I was still uncertain about was whether I should break it to them gently, or with a gun in my hand.

But then, the unexpected happened, and all my plans changed.

Esmeralda was standing beside me, still consumed with jubilation. Quite spontaneously, and quite abruptly, she reached out to me with both arms and embraced me. It was a long, tight embrace with little or no circumspection, as if she completely trusted me now. I felt her soft hair brushing against the stubble on my cheek and her perfect bosom pressing against my abdomen. No woman had genuinely touched me in that manner in a very long time. Before parting, she looked up at me, her eyes thoughtful and joyous, and perhaps something else...

"Thank you, Mister Jones," she said quietly, after a long pause. "For my father – for myself – I thank you. We would not have found the gold without you."

That was my first inkling that she might actually have a fondness for me, and it left me speechless. I stood there in

231

silence, noting that, when she moved on to Quinn, her embrace was not as enthusiastic, nor as long.

My eyes kept staring at the gold, but my mind was on something else now. My plans had been so clear before. Now, I wasn't sure. That one affectionate embrace had changed me, enough so, that I decided to keep my plans to myself, for now.

After relocating the horses and mules down to the gully, we spent several hours removing each ingot from the pit and arranging them in groups on the cavern floor. When we were finished, we counted two hundred and twelve of them.

It had been a long day, and this final exertion had left us exhausted. Collectively, we decided it would be best to wait until morning to load up the animals, and I decided I could wait until morning to tell my companions my real plans. Besides, I didn't relish sleeping with one eye open, and I would need my sleep if I planned on riding out of here in the morning – especially if I planned on riding out alone.

CHAPTER XVIII   Outlaws and Indians

It may have been the high altitude playing tricks on my mind that night, or perhaps the spirits of the ancient ones truly did visit us as we slept, but I dreamed of silent shadows moving throughout the cavern, dark shapes hovering over our sleeping forms and the stacked gold. And that may be why I was so startled that morning when I awoke and saw an Indian boy of perhaps ten-years-old standing in the entrance to the cave. He wore only breeches and had a tuft of shoulder-length black hair. Our eyes met, and I got the impression he was just as shocked to see me as I him, but by the time I got to my feet, he was gone.

"What is it?" Esmeralda asked, after I had shaken my companions awake.

"I saw an Indian boy," I answered. "And he saw us. Get your guns, and come with me."

"To go after a mere boy?" Quinn said doubtfully. "Maybe the runt got lost. Surely, a single boy is no threat to —"

"Where there are Indian children, there are Indian adults – and warriors, too, most likely. Now, get up and follow me."

Darting out of the cave, we looked all around us but he was nowhere to be seen.

"Let's go," I said. "Up to the citadel. Maybe we can see where he went from there."

"To what end, Jones?" Quinn said. "Shouldn't we just pack up the gold and get out of here?"

I did not answer but simply gestured for him and Esmeralda to follow me. If there were other Indians around, then the boy would certainly tell them about us. That meant, we'd be hounded for the rest of our journey. Seeing as how I was intending to journey alone, I did not want any curious Indians snooping around my campsites at night. I did not intend to harm the lad, only talk to him and satisfy the curiosity of his clansmen.

We climbed out of the gully and gained the village ruins, all the while looking out for the boy amidst the silent structures. When we reached a spot from which we could see the grassy plain below, I half-expected to see the boy far off in the distance, running away. We did not see the boy, but what we did see made Esmeralda cross herself, and Quinn and me curse out loud.

Less than one hundred yards from the outer ruins, and approaching the village, were two dozen horsemen, guns drawn, riding in a long line abreast. Beyond them, two horse-drawn, buckboard wagons followed about a half-mile behind. Even from this distance, it was evident that these were Martinique's men.

Our enemies had arrived, and they were looking for trouble.

They looked as though they were preparing to case the village. I did not think they had seen us yet, but staying put among these low rock walls was not an option in my mind.

"Quick!" I yelled to Quinn and Esmeralda. "Up to the citadel!"

Taking the path up to the high fortress would mean they would certainly see us, but we could defend ourselves much better from up there. And they did see us. We only managed to reach the safety of the wall at the top of the citadel moments before a scatter of bullets whizzed over our heads. Spreading out, we hunkered behind the wall with our rifles, like medieval archers preparing to defend a castle.

By the time I peeked over the edge, Martinique's men had dismounted and were approaching on foot, spread out among the ruins below. I counted twenty-two of them. As they darted from one cover to another, I picked out Martinique and Julio near the center of the group, but they moved too quickly between structures for me to get off a good shot.

"Don't shoot just yet," I said to Quinn five paces to my left, and Esmeralda five paces to my right, and they nodded back to me.

If I was not confident in my shot, then my companions could certainly hit nothing, and there was no sense tipping off our exact positions. I wanted the first shots to count, and the closer our enemies got, the better angle I would have on them, and the less their cover would conceal them.

When they were as close as I wished them to get, I decided it was time to let them know what they were up against. I picked out a fat, round-faced man in a red shirt who had carelessly taken cover behind a wall that was too small for him. His hat protruded above the stone works, and one arm carelessly flared out to the side. I would make an example of this fool. I would use him to put fear into the hearts of the others.

Placing the fat man's elbow in my sights, I squeezed the trigger. The man cried out as my bullet sliced through his arm, the report of my rifle echoing above the ruins. He clutched his bleeding wound, spinning around to sit against the wall, so that he could fit more of his body behind it, but I could still see his hat, and now I could see his booted feet sticking out on the ground beyond. His rifle had fallen into an open space about an arm's reach from where he sat.

"That's close enough, Martinique!" I shouted. "Tell your boys to back off, or we'll start putting holes in them!"

There was a long silence below, during which nothing moved and nothing could be heard but the whimpering of the wounded man. Finally, I heard the familiar French accent.

"I assume you have found it then?" Martinique called back, his voice more hopeful than fearful. "Tell me, Jones. Did you find it?"

I fired again, this time knocking the hat off the fat man's head, sending it flying off into the ruins beyond him. He hunkered lower after this, but it only gave me a better shot at his feet.

"That's no business of yours, Martinique!" I yelled. "And I told you to have your men back off."

"And if I refuse?" he asked in a surly tone.

My response was instantaneous. I fired again, and my bullet struck the fat man in his right foot, leaving a spattering of blood on the stones beyond. He wailed from the pain, his cries echoing off the rocks, and no doubt filling the ears of every one of Martinique's men, giving them a glimpse of what their fate might be should they come any closer. This unfortunate fool probably regretted ever riding with Martinique now, but I had little sympathy for him. By making an example of him, I hoped that much bloodshed could be avoided. I learned very soon, however, that Martinique was much better at making examples out of his men than I was.

My sights were steady on the squirming man, thus when Julio rose from his concealed position about fifteen yards further back, I did not have time to adjust my aim before Julio fired his six-gun twice and dropped back out of sight. He had not fired at me, but at the wounded man. His two bullets had killed the man instantly, bringing an abrupt and eternal end to the fat man's wailing.

So much for that idea.

"You have cost me a lot of time and expense, Mr. Jones," Martinique said. "You have proved quite a nuisance to me. Surely, you realize you cannot win. We outnumber you. You can't remain up there forever. I doubt you have enough ammunition to sustain you, should we attack, but nobody wants that. No one else needs to die here today, just like that old fool in the mission did not need to die. Miss Esmeralda must be grieving tremendously, the poor child.

You and Mister Quinn have brought her nothing but grief, Jones. Can't you see this?"

To my right, I heard Esmeralda mutter a curse in Spanish.

"I am not a bloodthirsty man," Martinique continued. "Nor am I a vengeful one. Though you have been an annoyance to me, Mister Jones, my offer still stands. If you throw in your lot with me, a share of that gold will be yours, and you can forget about being charged with the murder of a law-enforcement officer." He paused as if to let that sink in. Though I could not see him, I could imagine him shaking his head mockingly when he bellowed again. "Yes, in case you were wondering, poor old Sheriff Hobson died. You killed a peace officer who was in the execution of his duty, Mister Jones. Now, I'm afraid the murder of the priests will also fall on your head. It would be a pity to hang for something you did not do. It would be a pity to spend the rest of your life as an outlaw when you could live like a king."

I found it odd that Martinique was bargaining with me, for he really had no reason to. As he said, we were alone, outgunned, and in the middle of nowhere with no prospect for rescue. Then, it suddenly occurred to me that we were being intentionally distracted. Instinctively, I swung around to look behind me just in time to see a man climb over the wall on the opposite side of the escarpment.

While the citadel was surrounded by sharp cliffs, there were certain places where a skilled climber could scale up the side and gain the top. I could only assume Martinique, upon sighting us, had sent this man around to the far side of the rocky formation. The man was out of breath and covered in sweat from the arduous climb. He was absent hat, boots, and shirt, but he did wear a gun. When he noticed me looking in his direction, he went for it.

We fired simultaneously. My bullet struck him squarely in the face, obliterating his nose and knocking him back over the wall. If my bullet had not killed him, the fall surely did. But that was my last clear thought for a long time, because my bullet was not the only one to find its mark. His bullet grazed my head, millimeters away from being fatal, and knocked me senseless.

Seconds later, when I came to, I was on my hands and knees. My rifle was nowhere to be seen. Presumably, it had flown out of my hands and over the side. Blood trickled down my face. A sharp stinging sensation ran across my scalp from front to back.

A dissonance of gunfire filled the air. I could see that Quinn was firing his Winchester over the wall, and I could only assume Martinique's men were advancing on us. The ancient walls around me were alive with ricocheting lead.

Suddenly, Esmeralda was there, her soft hands cradling my blood-streaked face, concern in her eyes. She tore a length of cloth from the hem of her skirt and quickly wrapped it around my head as a bandage. I was still seeing stars, but I soon had enough sense to tell her where her priorities must now lie.

"Don't bother with me!" I roared, pushing her hand away. "Get that rifle and start shooting!"

For the briefest pause, she looked hurt by my outburst, but then quickly returned to her place at the wall, picked up the carbine, and joined Quinn in returning the fire. I was angry with myself, not at her. She had just happened to be unfortunate enough to be nearby. Martinique had played me for a fool. I had allowed him to out-maneuver me. It was an amateur's mistake, very unlike me. Perhaps Esmeralda was, in fact, partially to blame. For, lately, my usual clear-headed, calculating manner seemed to dither whenever she was around.

"There's too damned many of them!" Quinn shouted, ducking a fusillade of bullets meant for him. "Some of them are keeping our heads down, while the others advance!"

I managed to sit up and lean against the wall, catching my bearings for a few moments. During a lull in the incoming fire, I managed to peek over the edge and saw that at least ten of Martinique's men had made it to the base of the ramp leading up to the citadel. Before I had time to get a good look at them, their comrades forced my head down with a volley of well-aimed bullets.

"They're getting ready to rush us," I said to Quinn amid the gunfire. "How many do you count down there?"

"I don't know," the detective replied while hurriedly reloading the Winchester. "I'm not sure I've hit any. There may be twenty left."

"Listen," I said. "Give me your rifle, and take my gun."

Quinn looked at me sideways, as if wondering whether I was in my right mind, but he accepted my Peacemaker and handed me the Winchester.

"Get that Remington of yours ready, as well," I added. "Go wait at the top of the ramp, and stay out of sight. When you see them start up, wave to me. I'll keep a steady fire on them from here to make sure they move along quickly, right into the mouth of your guns. When they get to the top, set those guns ablazin' and let those bastards have it point-blank. Understand?"

His eyes went from my face to the rifle in my hands, as if questioning whether I could shoot it in my current state.

"Just make sure you do your part," he said. "There might be more men coming up that ramp than I have bullets."

I gave him a reassuring nod, and then he moved on, skirting along the escarpment about twenty paces from us until he was just at the head of the ramp, but still out of sight of those below.

Many bullets continued to strike the wall in front of me. I looked over at Esmeralda who was reloading the carbine. She gazed back at me uncertainly, as if she had misgivings about my plan. And she had good reason. The ramp was far off to our left. From our vantage point, we could fire on the ramp crossways, striking anyone climbing it from the side. But to make such a shot, we would not just have to raise our heads above the wall, we would have to lean out beyond it. During those few seconds, we would be the target of every gun down in the ruins. It was a nearly suicidal move, and that is precisely why I did not want Esmeralda to join me.

"I want you to go back up Quinn," I said to her firmly. "That carbine only holds one bullet anyway, and one bullet is not going to make the difference here. Back him up and cover him if he has to reload. Understand?"

I received no acknowledgment from her. She had been determined to hazard herself and join her rifle to mine, but she eventually acquiesced and ducked along the wall to join Quinn.

Still woozy from my concussion, and hoping I could stand up straight, much less shoot straight, I watched my companions, and waited for Quinn to give me the signal, but the signal never came.

Something had changed, something in the cacophony of gunfire below, as if there were more rifles firing now, but the new reports were further off. Then the whinny of horses and the thunder of hooves filled the air. Men shouted in alarm, intermixed with shrill yells that could only be Indian war cries. The withering fire against our wall had ceased, though the sound of the guns did not.

Venturing a look, I peered over the escarpment and saw complete chaos in the ruins below. Two dozen mounted Apache warriors rode in wild circles, kicking up a cloud of blinding red dust as they fired at Martinique's men. At first, I was elated by this sight, but then wondered at the futility of it all. I saw an Apache shot from his horse, and then another. The gunmen in the ruins had simply shifted their positions and were now firing at the Indians instead of us. The Indian attack, for all its valor, could have only one outcome. Martinique's men had the cover and the Apaches were in the open. It was only a matter of time before all the braves were knocked from their mounts.

Then, stranger still, the Apaches suddenly rode away. They wheeled their mounts in unison, as if the whole attack had been a planned feint, and withdrew from the ruins at full gallop. I was puzzled by this, that is, until the wind swept away the cloud of dust, and I realized that Martinique's wagons were no longer there. The two buckboards had still been climbing up the grassy slope to the ruins when the Indians had attacked, and now the braves had made off with both, leaving only the bullet-ridden bodies of the drivers to mark the spot where the wagons had been overrun.

The men below seemed to ascertain this at the same time I did. I heard an uproar of alarmed voices, Martinique's loudest of them all.

"Get after them! I need those damn wagons! A hundred dollars to every man if you bring back my wagons!"

As one, the gunmen below sprinted for their horses, disregarding us entirely now. It made sense from Martinique's perspective. He could deal with us anytime.

We weren't going anywhere. But if he did not have wagons to cart away the gold, he would have to wait at least a week for replacements.

Like the Indians, Martinique's men disappeared in a cloud of dust.

I thought I saw movement in the ruins, and squinted my eyes to try to ascertain how many men had been left behind, but a sudden wave of nausea came over me and I had to sit down. The earlier bullet may have only grazed me, but the effects of its concussion were lingering. I felt suddenly dizzy. I fought it, but to no avail. The feeling rapidly worsened until I vomited onto the rocks beside me, each heave sending a pulsing pain through my head, each one growing in intensity.

Then, finally, I blacked out.

CHAPTER XIX   For Valor's Sake

Esmeralda's hands were caressing my face when I came to again. She was kneeling over me, and smiled when she saw recognition in my eyes. I tried to sit up, but she gently pushed me back.

"You must rest," she said.

"How long have I been out?"

"A few minutes."

"Are they gone?" I could see we were still atop the citadel, and I was exactly where I had fallen. Then, I suddenly realized we were alone. "Where's Quinn?"

"He is gone," she said, with averted eyes. "He went below to the ruins."

"He did what?" I grabbed her arms and hauled myself upright, ignoring the splitting pain in my head.

"He said he could see where Martinique was hiding, and believed him to be with only one or two other men. He said he thought he could sneak up on them and end this whole thing in one moment. He took your pistol with him. I tried to stop him, but he said it's what you would have done." She shook her head. "I lost sight of him when he reached the village. A short time later, I heard three gunshots. I have heard nothing since."

"The damn fool!" I muttered, rising to my knees to look down at the village below. It appeared as empty as it had been when we arrived. Far off on the plain, a large swirl of dust marked the location of Martinique's men, embroiled in a fight with the Apaches, the sporadic gunfire just audible above the wind.

I examined the ruins, tried to discern anything I could, but I saw no one. "Damn it!" I cursed again. "That eastern bastard did just what they wanted him to. He walked right into their trap."

As I was contemplating what to do next, I met eyes with Esmeralda, and it was apparent she knew what I was thinking.

"No," she pleaded fervently, grabbing hold of my hands. "You must not go down there. You must not!"

I held her hands in mine for a long moment, then folded them together and placed them back in her lap. "There's no other way," I said, picking up the Winchester. "Quinn was right. It's what I would have done. While those cowboys are off fighting the Indians, we have a chance to kill Martinique. Once they return, it'll all be over."

"Then I am coming, too," she said resolutely, grabbing the carbine.

"No. You can help better from up here. Once I'm down in those ruins, I won't be able to see what's on the other side of the next pile of stones. Watch me from up here, and fire off a shot if you see anyone closing in on me."

After some hesitation, she agreed to this, and embraced me one last time before letting me go.

"Take up a position here," I instructed her. "When I start down the ramp, fire off one shot at the ruins. That might distract them long enough for me to get down there."

I knew it was crazy, that our unseen enemies had the advantage, that, if they were watching – and I knew they were – they would see me coming down the ramp, and would probably kill me before I reached any cover. It would be a good thirty-yard sprint, but it was all downhill.

When I was ready, I nodded back at Esmeralda, and she fired the carbine. Instantly, I bounded down the slope two steps at a time. I held the Winchester in one hand, for I had no delusions about using it until I had reached the ruins. Half-way down, I heard another gunshot. I did not know if Esmeralda had reloaded in record time, or if the gun had been fired at me, but it had the effect of throwing off my timing. I lost my footing on a jutting rock and rolled head over heels the rest of the way down. This got me to the base of the ramp quickly, but at the cost of many bruises and a nearly unbearable pain in my head.

Despite my discomfort, I scrambled to the nearest cover, a half-crumbled wall that had once been the side of a building, and remained there for several minutes, catching my breath and allowing the pain in my head to somewhat subside.

I could see Esmeralda looking over the wall high above me, saw her wave, and waved back to show her I was okay. But when she kept gesticulating, I studied her more closely and realized she was pointing, swooping her hand up and over, as if to indicate someone had moved close to me and was just on the other side of the wall.

Sure enough, as I held my breath to listen, I heard the solid heel of a boot carefully stepping onto the gravel to my left. Whoever was there was trying to sneak up on me. Perhaps my opponents believed I had broken my neck in the tumble and had sent someone to verify I was incapacitated. Perhaps it was Martinique himself. Or perhaps it was Quinn, safe and sound and trying to contact me. But I could discern none of these from Esmeralda's hand signals, and so I decided the non-lethal end of my rifle was the right choice.

The boots drew closer. I waited until I was certain he would wheel around the corner in the next step, and then I moved. I stepped towards the wall's edge, brought my rifle up, and thrust the butt-end forward just as a head appeared around the corner. The stock made solid contact, smashing his nose to a pulp, rattling three teeth from his head, and knocking him out cold in a single blow.

I stood back somewhat in shock, and somewhat regretting the vehemence of the blow, for my victim's face would never look the same again. Had it been Martinique, this would not have bothered me in the least. But it was not Martinique, nor was it Quinn.

It was young Jesse.

The young man, whose life was being led to errant ways by Martinique and his bunch, now lay there motionless, his face covered in blood, the shotgun he had been holding lying across his body. Had he intended to use the shotgun on me? Was it not enough that Martinique had sent this kid along as an accomplice to the priests' murders, that he now used the boy to kill his opponents? The thought angered me.

I dragged the rest of Jesse behind the cover with me. As I did so, I got a good look down the alley from which the boy had come, and something caught my eye, something that confirmed my worst fears.

Some thirty paces away, partially hidden by another wall, a body lay upon the ground. From where I knelt, it was only visible from the waist down, but the wool trousers and the knee-high boots were as distinct as the upside-down derby hat lying upon the rocky path. The legs were motionless.

I did not even look back at Esmeralda to see if the path ahead of me was clear, I simply crept forward, holding the Winchester at the ready, my eyes locked on the still form. When I finally turned the corner, I saw that my comrade was indeed dead. He looked as many of my own opponents had looked after a duel in the street, his arms out-stretched, his mouth open, his lifeless eyes staring at the sky past crooked spectacles, a red splotch in the center of his chest where the mortal bullet had struck, my own pistol and his Remington lying a few feet away. No one would ever question his valor now.

He was obviously shot from directly ahead, and presumably by an opponent at which he himself was about to shoot, but then I looked closer at his hands, and noticed something that made me fume with anger. Initially, I had dismissed the blood-stains there, since it was very likely he clutched his chest before dying. But now I saw that the blood stemmed from wounds. On one hand, his middle fingers were nearly severed. The other was pierced through the palm. These wounds, coupled with Esmeralda's recounting three distinct shots, revealed to me precisely what had happened. It was clear that the man who had killed Quinn had taunted him in his last moments, shooting the guns out of Quinn's hands before placing the fatal round in the direct center of his chest.

I knew only one man among Martinique's crew who could manage such a cold and calculated execution. It was as clear to me as if he had signed his name across Quinn's corpse. And then, I realized I must have still been suffering from the effects of my concussion, because I had just done an incredibly foolish thing.

"Hello, amigo," I heard Julio say.

Out of the corner of my eye, to my left, I saw Julio standing at the end of the alley, very likely in the same spot from which he had gunned down Quinn. I knew his pistol was leveled at me. My Winchester was in my left hand. There was no way I could point it toward the expert gunman before he put a bullet through my head.

"Put down the rifle, amigo," Julio said, as if reading my thoughts.

I did as he asked, then slowly turned my head that I might see his face. He smiled widely, as a fisherman who had just hooked a fish.

"Your friend was slow," he said jovially. "He did not belong out here."

I knew he was trying to anger me. It was a common ploy used by gunfighters before a duel. But this was not a duel, and he had the upper hand.

"Why don't you get on with it, Jose," I replied, intentionally using his real name.

"Now you are just being rude, amigo. I would like nothing more than to kill you, but Mister Martinique wants to know where the gold is first."

"You can tell him to go to hell!"

His pistol erupted in a loud shot that sent another bullet into Quinn's body.

"You're a son of a bitch, Jose!" I grimaced, but did not move.

"There you go again, amigo, being rude." He cocked the revolver again. "Do you want your friend to go home to his family looking like himself, or a slab of meat? Where is the gold, amigo?"

I was about to respond with a vulgarity, when another voice spoke from atop the wall.

"Drop the gun!" It was Esmeralda. She crouched on the wall ten feet to Julio's right, pointing the carbine directly at his head.

She must have seen Julio lying in ambush, and, rather than fire a warning shot, which probably would have resulted in Julio stepping out and killing me outright, she had come down from the citadel to turn the tables on him.

Julio's smile faded. "You are making a mistake, senorita."

"Be silent, murderer!" she spat. "You will hang for what you have done!"

She should have killed him right then and there, and taken a chance that the final spasm of his hand would not result in my death, but she did not. I could see the doubt in her eyes, and I knew Julio could hear it in her voice.

Then another voice spoke, this one from the ruins just to my front. "Go ahead, my dear." Martinique emerged from the shadows holding a small revolver which he pointed at me. "Go ahead and shoot, and Mister Jones will be killed in the next instant."

"Do it!" I prompted her.

"Do you wish another man's soul to be on your conscience, my dear?" Martinique countered. "For, I assure you, Mister Jones here will need a great degree of absolution if he is ever to reach paradise. Do you want that?" He pressed her more forcefully. "Do you, Miss Esmeralda?"

She did not take her eyes from Julio, but I could see them blink. She cared for me, and Martinique had gotten to her.

"No," she said quietly. "But I will shoot, if there is no other way."

"Oh, but there is, my dear, there is. The gold is hidden somewhere in these ruins, and you know where it is. Now, I have enough dynamite on my wagons to blow this place to kingdom come searching for it, but I have no desire to do that. It would be such a waste. So, I will make you a proposal. Put the weapon down, and lead me to the gold. When I see it before my eyes, when I can touch it with my hands, you and Mister Jones may go free. No harm will come to either of you. All I want is the gold."

"Don't listen to him, Esmeralda!" I said, but I knew my pleas were futile. I could already see the hope in her eyes that Martinique might live up to his word. Some hope is better than none. It was certain that, should the guns start firing, Julio would die first, followed immediately by me, and that would leave Esmeralda holding an unloaded, single-shot carbine facing Martinique who held a six-shot revolver.

The distant gun battle that had been raging between Martinique's men and the Apaches diminished considerably at that moment, and a broad smile crossed Martinique's face.

"Whatever decision you make, my dear, I hope you will make it quickly. The wagons should be here soon, and I would very much like to load up the gold and leave this place."

"Do you give your word that no harm will come to Mister Jones?" she asked feebly, her tone communicating just how much value she placed on Martinique's word.

"You have my word of honor, miss – my word as a Frenchman."

After a slight nod, Esmeralda lowered the carbine and leaned it against the wall.

"Excellent!" Martinique said with delight, crossing over to her while Julio kept his gun on me. "Shall we, my dear? You may lead the way."

Esmeralda cast a dismal look at me, still on my knees beside Quinn's body. Then she turned and headed towards the gully. As Martinique followed her, he glanced once over his shoulder at Julio, and I saw an unspoken communication take place. The fake smile was briefly absent from the Frenchman's face, and I knew what he intended for Julio to do.

"Well," I said to Julio, after they had left. "That bastard is not going to keep his word. You and I both know that."

"The girl does not know," Julio replied.

"She does. She just didn't have any other choice. So, what are you waiting for, a signal from your boss?"

He nodded, though his expression indicated there was more to it than that. There was an inner turmoil of some kind going on inside the gunfighter's head. I had a hunch I knew what he truly wanted, and it wasn't a share of the gold.

"You know, it's a shame," I said in a resigned tone.

"What?"

"We were on different sides all those years down in New Mexico, and we never found out who was better – who was faster. Surely, you must ponder that, too, sometimes."

"I think about it all the time, amigo. It is the only reason you are still alive. I could have killed you many times. I have killed men in cold blood before, like your friend there. They mean nothing to me. But you, amigo – you are different." Julio then sighed heavily. "I am afraid Mister Martinique will not let you live."

I smiled audaciously. "Then maybe it is time."

Our eyes met, and it was clear that Julio understood my meaning. He nodded graciously, almost expectantly, as if he had planned for this outcome all along. There were some things more important than gold, after all.

"Pick it up," he gestured to my Peacemaker, while keeping his own gun pointed at me. "Pick it up very slowly, amigo, and holster it."

I did as he said.

"Now stand up," he said.

When I had squared up with him, he holstered his own weapon, and then smiled. "Just like old times. Eh, amigo?"

There was a hint of anxiety in his tone, something that was not there when he had faced other men. The fingers that had been rock-steady when facing Thomas in the saloon, now flittered a few inches above his weapon as if he were playing some unseen instrument. His eyes cut to my face and my gun hand alternately. Something inside him did not want to be there, yet he had to be there. He could not help himself. Like a man venturing too close to the edge of a cliff, he had to know, even if the pursuit of that knowledge would lead to his own demise. He was nervous, and he should have been, because I already knew the answer to that great question that had hung over us for so long.

I saw his eyes skip a blink, and the fingers change their rhythm, and I knew the next instant his weapon would be in his hand, so I went for my own. The Peacemaker and my hand melded as naturally as if they were two magnets. Then it fired, marring the air between Julio and me with a lingering white smoke. It did not need to fire again. It did not, because I was faster than Julio, I had always been faster – and I had always known it.

When the smoke cleared, Julio was still standing, but his knees were buckling. His gun was in his hand, but he had not yet fired it, nor would he ever again. His jaw hung open as if in confusion, a guttural noise emanating with his final breath. Where his left eye had been, there was now an oozing hole, and the stones behind him were painted crimson.

The next moment, Jose "Julio" Hernandez, the notorious gunman of the New Mexico Territory, the desperate outlaw wanted for countless murders, whose very name had struck fear in the hearts of adversaries and innocents, toppled to the ground, dead.

CHAPTER XX   Yellow Iron

I ran to the gully, not looking back, the thunder of hooves filling my ears. Riders were approaching from the far side of the ruins and I did not wish them to see me. I bounded down the slope and into the sandy bottom, trusting that the trees lining the bank would hide me fairly well from anyone looking down from the ruins.

I ran as fast as I could, feeling my head pulsing with every step, hoping to overtake and kill Martinique, and then escape with Esmeralda on our own horses.

When I reached the entrance to the cave, I was relieved to find our horses and mules hitched outside just where we had left them, but I had not encountered Esmeralda or Martinique, and that disturbed me. Concluding that they must already be inside the cave, I stood to the side of the entrance and listened intently. I heard nothing.

This was an unfavorable situation, since I would have to expose myself to peer inside the dark cavity, and such a move would surely be fatal if Martinique was in there waiting for me. There was no telling how long I had before Martinique's returning men found this place. As I saw it, I was left with only one option.

"Martinique!" I called. "Are you in there?"

After a brief silence, I heard a woman gasp as if in pain. I instantly ducked inside, gun drawn, determined to save her or die, then stopped in my tracks when I saw both Martinique and Esmeralda standing before me amongst the piles of gold ingots. She was in front of the Frenchman, wincing as he held her arms behind her and nudged the muzzle of his revolver under her jaw.

"Put the gun down, Jones," he said with a sinister smile.

I would have had no trouble putting a bullet through his brain at this range, but his pistol was cocked and ready to fire, and the last twitch of his finger might blast a hole through Esmeralda's neck. I had no choice. I did as he said.

"Okay," I said. "Now, let her go, Martinique. You've got the gold. You've got what you want. Let her go."

"Move over there," he said, pointing to the empty pit from which we had exhumed the gold.

After I had moved to the edge of the pit, he grinned and shoved Esmeralda at me so hard that I had to reach out and grab her to stop her from falling into the hole. As she regained her footing in my arms, I saw gratefulness in her eyes, but sadness, too. For we both understood Martinique's intentions. He would never let us go.

Outside the cave, horses could be heard drawing up. Martinique's men seemed to have had no trouble finding it. Perhaps they had seen me running up the gully. Soon the cavern would be full of his henchmen.

"Is your word worth anything?" I said, in a futile appeal to Martinique's honor. "Your word as a Frenchman!"

"I have only one country, Jones, and its name is gold."

"Then kill me if you must, but spare her. Give her safe passage back to Dougson. She will agree to keep quiet about the gold. That's all I ask."

Martinique gave me a clear enough answer by extending his arm and aiming the pistol at us.

"No," he snarled. "You have made me mad, Jones, madder than I've been in years, and I don't allow that from any man. You have dug your own grave, and now you shall lie in it." He smiled smugly, and added in a sardonic tone, "Who knows? Someday your rotting skeletons may be unearthed still locked in that embrace. How touching."

His face drew grave again as he steadied the gun on me. My mind raced for some means of stopping him, but he was too far away for me to lurch at him, and any move would surely result in him adjusting his aim and killing Esmeralda.

Then, a shot rang out, and the cavern was instantly filled with thick gun smoke and the aroma of black powder. I glanced at Esmeralda to see if she was hit, for I felt no wounds on me. She appeared just as confused as I was.

As the smoke began to clear, we saw Martinique now lying face down on the ground, the gun still clutched in his hand. He did not move, nor did he breathe. As the smoke cleared further, I saw two figures beyond Martinique's still form standing in the cave entrance. One wielded a long gun with a smoking muzzle. The gun was an old musket, a long musket, and it was held by an Apache warrior with a bandaged arm.

It was Long Musket. He had fired the shot. He had killed Martinique. The other warrior was Red Vest. Both Apaches gazed back at us with triumph and resolve in their eyes. I had wrongly assumed it was Martinique's men on those horses outside. Clearly, it had been the Apaches. The Indians had been victorious in their fight with the gunmen.

Despite this success, Long Musket still looked brooding and severe. The young brave walked over to me, said a few words in Apache, then turned and marched out, leaving Red Vest behind to translate.

"My nephew says, two nights ago, he tried to steal your woman, that he might return her to you. Then his debt to you would be repaid."

"Oh," I replied, as though that made perfect sense. In truth, it seemed ridiculous to me that a man would steal something only so that he could give it back, but this was not the time nor the company in which to voice such an opinion. At least, I now had some explanation for Long Musket's late-night visitation. "Well, today he saved our lives, and I'm much obliged to him for that."

"He did not want to," Red Vest said. I could see a slight smile on his face in the dim light. "Things are right between you now. When next you meet, do not expect him to be as generous."

I nodded. "All the same, please give him my thanks."

We returned to the ruins. The afternoon wind whistled through the stone structures as if to carry off the spirits of the dead. The Apache warriors sifted through the belongings and saddlebags of the slain. The braves were covered in the red dust stirred up in their fight with the gunmen, and several bore wounds which they seemed to ignore. Their blood was still up from the battle, and they looked at Esmeralda and me with murderous faces, as if they would like nothing more than to add two more victims to their slaughter.

There was, however, one exception to these grim visages. The Apache boy I had seen at the mouth of the cave earlier that morning was there, jumping from one rock wall to the other, smiling back at us and laughing playfully, saying things in his language that I could not understand.

The braves left us alone, whether by Red Vest's direction, or the mere fact that we were enemies of Martinique, I never knew. I did discover, however, that Red Vest's band had been shadowing both our party and that of Martinique as we had made our trek across the plain. Apparently, Martinique – or Maha-neek – had risen to the level of devil chief in the Apaches' minds after committing an untold number of insults and infractions on the reservation over the years. Red Vest had decided to put an end to his arrogance, and had carefully chosen the moment to strike, when Martinique's wagons were separated from his horsemen. In chasing the wagons, Martinique's men had ridden directly into a carefully staged ambush. Red Vest had brought twenty-two painted warriors with him, half of whom he hid in the tall grass on the plain. When the hired guns rode past them in pursuit of the wagons, the trap was sprung and the fate of the horsemen sealed.

Now, all but one of Martinique's men lay dead, the lone survivor, young Jesse. He sat on the ground guarded by two braves, his nose swollen and crooked, his face bloody and bruised, his eyes full of fear. After some deliberations, I convinced Red Vest to spare him. He was just a boy, after all.

Soberly, Esmeralda and I returned to the alley where the bodies of Quinn and Julio lay – one whose time had come too soon, the other's long overdue. Our victory was not even bittersweet. It was simply bitter, and hollow.

As we knelt beside Quinn's body, I could not help but gaze upon his outstretched, mangled hands and remember that tune I heard him play in the saloon on the day we met. I reached out and placed his arms across his chest while Esmeralda whispered a prayer in Spanish. We would see that his body received proper treatment, and made it home to his next of kin. He would, no doubt, be buried with honors, a detective who had died in the line of duty.

Julio, however, would not receive such ceremony. Like so many notorious gunfighters before him, he would be buried in an unmarked grave. Surely the families of his victims would desecrate his grave otherwise. His face was still frozen in that last instant of life, the moment when he realized I had beaten him. Oddly, that image would come to haunt me in later years, not out of any remorse for Julio, but out of regret for the life I had lived. In time, the faces of the men I had killed eventually faded from my memory, but Julio's never did, as if he, my last victim, represented them all, and the guilt I would carry for the rest of my life.

As Esmeralda continued to pray over Quinn's body, I looked up to see Red Vest standing only a few paces away, watching with sympathy, not indifference.

"He was your brother?" he asked grimly.

"Yes," I said solemnly.

Red Vest nodded, and said no more, as if he did not need to know any more.

Horses whinnied at the edge of the ruins. A few of the braves were tending to the captured horses. I saw that they had placed Carondelet, Don Carlos, and Ulysses among them. As I was trying to come up with the right words to ask this Apache chief if he intended to give them back to me, a high-pitched voice cried out from the citadel above us. We both looked up to see the Apache boy, standing on the rock wall along the cliff's edge, waving to get Red Vest's attention and pointing out at the plains beyond.

I followed Red Vest up to the top of the wind-swept escarpment to see what the boy had spied. A stir of dust marked the grassy plain about a dozen miles away. I did not have to stare at it for long before I discerned the shades of blue, riding in pairs, stretched out in a long column, a red and white flag whipping from a standard at its head.

It was the cavalry. Major Garrett's troop was coming. They had either found the tracks left by Martinique's party, or had been keyed off by the sounds of the gun battle, but it was clear their destination was Ciudadela. They were pushing their horses hard, and would likely be here within the hour.

It sounds cold-hearted, with bodies of allies and enemies lying about, but I saw an opportunity in this, a golden one – and I took it.

"You and your braves had best ride on," I said to Red Vest, with some measure of urgency, pointing at the approaching column. "We don't want some greenhorn trooper shooting one of your braves, either on-purpose or by accident. Don't worry. We'll explain everything to them, how Martinique's men attacked you, and you had no choice but to defend yourselves. If they don't believe me, they'll believe the woman. You had best take your fallen braves with you."

Red Vest made no movement whatsoever. He simply stared back at me, his face like stone.

"Well," I said more fervently. "Go on. Get out of here. Do you want to have another war on your hands?"

But again, Red Vest did not move.

Remember when I mentioned it was foolish to lie to an Indian? Whether it was my odd demeanor, or just a general distrust in the white man, Red Vest clearly saw right through me.

"Jones speaks with a forked tongue," he said finally. "Wants to keep yellow iron for himself."

Traditionally the Apaches had little use for such treasures, but Red Vest clearly understood the value of the so-called "yellow iron" down in the cave below. Perhaps, the Apache chief had known what Martinique was after all along. The Indians had spying webs of their own. They had to. Though we were at peace, they did not trust the white-eyes, and had to keep abreast of army troop movements, or the next lay of railroad tracks, or the next "legal" land grab.

Before I could come up with a response, Esmeralda joined us on the summit. She eyed me suspiciously, as if she, too, knew from my manner that I had been double-dealing. Was I that transparent to her? Perhaps my age was catching up with me, and I wasn't as good at playing these games as I once had been. Or perhaps I was getting tired of death following me everywhere. When I looked into

Esmeralda's eyes, I felt like a boy with only two pennies hopelessly eyeing a ten-dollar toy, and I wished I was a better man.

"You're right," I said to Red Vest, finally making up my mind. "The gold rightfully belongs to your people. That was the wish of Father Perez. But if those troopers get wind of it, you'll not get an ounce, and you'll have a gold rush on your hands. An army of prospectors and freebooters will come here chasing the dream. They'll turn your country upside-down looking for similar treasures, and when they don't find it, they'll be just as bad as Martinique, or worse."

Esmeralda looked at me contentedly, as if I had just put her waking suspicions to rest. But I had not fooled Red Vest. Though he said nothing, his expression clearly indicated he knew my sudden change of heart was for the sake of expediency.

"Those cavalry boys aren't going to believe your story," I continued brazenly. "Not for one minute."

"I know," he replied.

"To ride off would only confirm your guilt."

"I know," he said again, after a long pause, this time eyeing me sagaciously. For, I had advised him to do that very thing only moments ago.

"There is a way we can stop the troopers from finding the gold," I said.

"How?"

I glanced at the wagons his braves had parked near the edge of the ruins and nodded.

"It will take a long time to load them," he said, clearly unimpressed. "Wagons move slow."

"I'm not suggesting we try to carry the gold away. I say we leave it right here. We just make it so the soldiers can't find it."

After a few seconds, I saw a wave of comprehension cross his face. His lips pursed in a small smile, and I knew he understood my meaning. He then pointed at the captive Jesse, still under guard down by the ruins.

"What about him? The boy's tongue will be a poison in the soldiers' ears."

The youth was too far away to hear our conversation, but he was observing our every move, clearly fearful that we were mulling over his fate.

"Leave him to me," I said, drawing my Bowie knife from its sheath. "Do you give me his life?"

With raised eyebrows, the Apache chief nodded, apparently surprised that even I would take such extreme measures.

As I began to descend the ramp, eyeing the frightened youth below, Esmeralda ran after me, tugging at my arm. "Don't do it!" she pleaded. "You will regret it. He is just a boy!"

I stopped and turned to face her, holding her hands between us. "Don't worry, Esmeralda," I said in a reassuring tone, not loud enough for the boy to hear. "Don't worry."

Then, as she stood there, looking back at me in confusion, I spun on my heel and marched directly for Jesse, all the while holding the knife before me and glaring at the youth with a venomous stare. He whimpered as I drew near, and fell over into the fetal position, his limbs quite paralyzed with fear.

I pulled his head up by the hair, and held the knife to his throat, letting him feel the cold blade against his skin.

"Now, you listen to me, you little son of a bitch," I snarled. "You will never tell anyone what happened here, for as long as you live. Is that clear? You know who I am. You know what I can do!"

He nodded briskly.

"Say it!"

"Y-Yes, Mister Jones," he muttered between bloody lips.

"If I hear you ever talked, if I hear you ever rode with the likes of Martinique again, I will hunt you down and slaughter you like a pig. And I will find you! Now, get out of here! Take the gully to the west and stay out of sight of the soldiers. Got it?"

"Y-Yes, Mister Jones."

After sheathing my knife on my belt, I pulled the youth to his feet, then added in a slightly less vehement tone. "Go home, boy. Go home, and stay out of trouble."

Like a condemned criminal just granted a pardon, Jesse sighed with relief, then turned and ran off to retrieve his horse from the captured lot. As I watched him ride away, kicking his horse down the sandy wash as if it could not go fast enough, I was not sure I had done the smartest thing in letting him go. Rotten apples seldom turn fresh, and it would not be the first time I had let an enemy go only to rue the decision later.

"Thank you," I heard Esmeralda say behind me. Then I felt her gentle arms wrap around my waist, and her face lean flat against my back.

And I knew I had done the right thing.

CHAPTER XXI   Epilogue

I am old now.

On cold winter days like this one, I feel my age in my bones, in my joints, a body pushed hard over a lifetime on the western frontier. The great San Francisco mountains still peek their white heads over the horizon at me, the forests and high desert are just as vast, but there are now towns and settlements where there once had been trading posts and, in some places, nothing at all. So many have come here, so many from the east, and I suppose, a generation from now, many more will have come.

So, reader, you are probably wondering what happened to Father Castillo's gold and all the players in my tale. I will start by telling you, as I write this last chapter, I have just exchanged an affectionate smile with my loving wife, who is down in the garden just now, on her hands and knees, nurturing her precious tomatoes. Her hair is now streaked with more gray than black, but she is as beautiful to me as the first time I saw her. Esmeralda and I have lived a blessed life in this land we have come to love. Our ranch sits in a meadow of rich soil under the lee of a sleeping volcano called Mount Elden. It is a short ride from

Flagstaff, close enough to just hear the whistles of the trains arriving after their three-hundred-mile journey across the high desert from Albuquerque. We've kept a moderate herd of cattle over the years, but not enough to give us trouble, or to be a threat to any other rancher. Here, on this pristine land, we raised three boys and a girl, all of whom have long since come of age and ventured off to make their own fortunes in the world.

The old mission in Dougson was rebuilt, in no small part due to the contributions of an anonymous donor who insisted it be renamed the Perez-Garcia Mission. That anonymous donor, of course, was my lovely wife, who makes a trip there once a year to visit her father's grave in the mission cemetery.

Along with the joy and blessings, we've had our share of trials and tragedies, but our love has been constant throughout.

Now, after reading thus far, you have probably concluded we kept all the gold to ourselves, and that I am just another deceitful white-eye who cheated the Indians out of what rightfully belongs to them. But that could not be further from the truth.

That day, at Ciudadela, the noise of the gunfight had drawn the attention of Major Garrett's cavalry, but just before the horse soldiers arrived, one final explosion shook the earth. The column scattered for cover, and it took us some time to convince the troopers they were not under attack, before they finally rose from their positions and approached. The major surveyed the scene with raised eyebrows. The dead lay everywhere. It goes without saying, we had to do some fancy talking to persuade him we had simply protected the Indian cultural site from Martinique and his band of looters, who had become belligerent when denied access to the old ruins. We further explained that the explosion the major had heard was a stick of dynamite lit off by one of Martinique's dying men, in a last desperate act. I could see suspicion in the major's eyes, but he did not question our account of the events. It helped that Red Vest and the major had met before, and that the major seemed to have some measure of respect for the Apache chief. Though Red Vest's English was broken, I discovered he was a much better liar than I was. Still, Major Garrett was no fool. He may not have voiced his thoughts, but he had been around this territory long enough to know what Martinique had really been after. The bodies were collected for burial, and placed in shallow graves for later retrieval by their next of kin. The major then ordered his troop to conduct a thorough search of the ruins, under the pretense of ensuring no valuables were left behind. When this search turned up nothing, it clearly did little to allay his suspicions, but he pressed the matter no further. Eventually, we bade farewell to Red Vest and his band. The Apaches departed, and Esmeralda and I accompanied the cavalry on the long ride back to Dougson, a long train of horses behind us bearing the empty saddles of the dead.

The soldiers had not found anything in their search of the ruins because that last explosion had not, in fact, been lit off by one of Martinique's men, but by me. The carefully-placed dynamite had closed up the cave's entrance quite thoroughly, such that, when the dust settled, no one would have known it had been there at all.

Two days later, while Esmeralda and I were explaining our story for the hundredth time to the new acting-sheriff of Dougson, Red Vest returned to Ciudadela with many more braves, and, under cover of darkness, unearthed the hidden gold, spiriting it away to some hiding place on the reservation, of which I was completely ignorant and wish to remain so to the end of my days. Exactly one month later, Esmeralda and I met Red Vest in secret to receive our portion as we had previously agreed. Our share was only a fraction of the horde, but it was substantial enough to set us up properly. Esmeralda agreed to accept it only if we made a substantial donation to the church – and, thus, the mission was rebuilt.

I must admit I was somewhat surprised Red Vest had let us have any of the gold – surprised and ashamed. Ashamed, because I might not have done the same. He gave me a second surprise that day, too, presenting me with my father's rifle that I had dropped over the side of the citadel. It was damaged beyond repair and would never fire again, but the gift was most moving. I keep it now over the fireplace.

Of young Jesse, I am sad to say, the lad met his end several years later after a drunken brawl in a saloon down in Yuma. He was shot dead by another inebriated fool who, in turn, was strung up not long after. It is so difficult for a youngster to find the straight and narrow path when he's been led astray from the start. I must admit, I myself was saved only by the patient counseling of my devoted wife. Had she not changed my course, I am certain my end would have been similar to Jesse's.

After the fight at the Ciudadela ruins, I never drew my gun again. Some years later, I stopped wearing one altogether. I have adopted, to some extent, the late detective Quinn's axiom, that one should not appear to be looking for trouble. Perhaps, I should have at least attempted to help

Jesse return to the fold. In recent years, I have come to regret that I did not.

The young Apache Long Musket, whose real name I later learned was *Bodaway*, which translates to something like *Firestarter*, never rid of himself of the anger and hatred he harbored towards the whites. His was a short life, full of quarrels and violence. He ran with the Apache Kid, was wanted for cattle rustling, and was eventually killed down south of the border in a shootout with Mexican soldiers.

And, finally, there is Red Vest, whose real name is not Red Vest, but he wished me to call him that after he learned it was my name for him. Though we come from different people, with different backgrounds and different cultures, we are bonded by our memories of how this land used to be, and we have developed a special friendship over the years, to the point that I am as welcome in his house, as he is in mine. We have helped each other on many occasions, and there are few secrets between us.

He never speaks of Long Musket. Whether he is simply honoring an Apache tradition regarding the dead, or his nephew's tragic life is simply too painful to discuss, I do not know, nor do I intend to ask him. There are boundaries even close friends must not cross.

Until two years ago, when the rheumatism in my aging joints prevented it, Red Vest and I hunted elk together every winter. Now, he comes to visit me, and quite often. He putters up the drive in his Ford Model T, of which he is enormously proud, the cotton tunic and red vest long since replaced by a proper suit and tie. He has spent many hours trying to explain to me the workings of the automobile, but my aging mind has no desire to comprehend it. Esmeralda and I shall never own one. We still prefer the silent tranquility of our horses. But I admire Red Vest, perhaps more than I do any man. He is a true survivor. He does not resist the winds of change, but lets them fill his sails and propel him to new and wonderful things. Though he is several years my senior, I believe he will still be crossing the desert in that noisy contraption long after I am in my grave.

We often sit on the veranda in our rocking chairs, splitting a bottle, two old men reminiscing about the freedom and excitement of the old days. We gaze out at the vista as the sun sets, feeling the cold gusts whipping off the plains and buffeting our ears.

Sometimes, I think I hear voices on that wind, echoes of the ancients, of the Apache and Navajo, of conquistadors and missionaries, of settlers, soldiers, and cowboys. I think on days long gone, days that will never come again, when men were known for their speed, their courage, or their cowardice.

My name is Elijah Jones. When I was young, I lived in the age of the gun...

THE END